THE DAY OF SMALL THINGS

THE DAY OF SMALL THINGS

John Attenborough

'Who hath despised the day of small things?'
Zechariah 4, 10

Hodder & Stoughton
LONDON SYDNEY AUCKLAND

First published in Great Britain in 1994
by Hodder And Stoughton Ltd

10 9 8 7 6 5 4 3 2 1

British Library Cataloguing in Publication Data

Attenborough, John
Day of Small Things
I.   Title
823.914 [F]

ISBN 0-340-60175-2

Typeset by Keyboard Services, Luton

Printed in Great Britain by
Mackays of Chatham PLC, Chatham, Kent

Hodder And Stoughton Ltd
A division of Hodder Headline PLC
47 Bedford Square
London WC1B 3DP

To
MOLLY WALTER
who was the first of my friends
to visit Melbridge
and overhear the gossip
about the Selby marriage

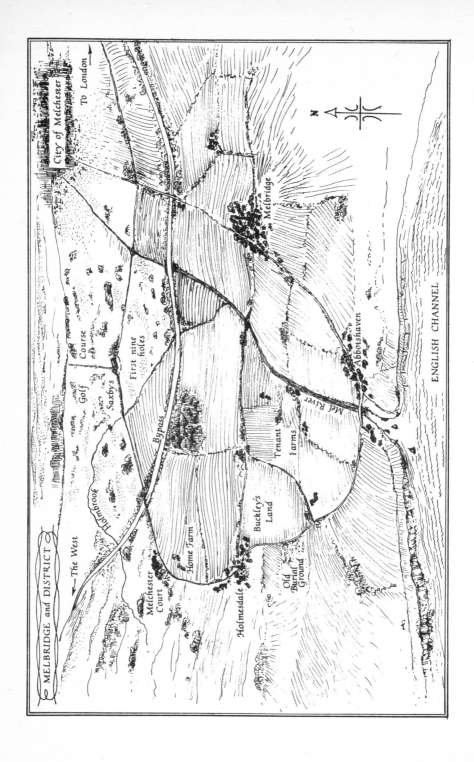

MELBRIDGE and DISTRICT

The West —

City of Melchester

To London

MELCHESTER

N

Holmbrook

Saxby's

Golf
Course

First nine
holes

Bypass

Melchester
Court

Home Farm

Holmesdale

Buckley's
Land

Old
Burial
Ground

Tenant
Farms

Melbridge

Mel River

Abbotshaven

ENGLISH CHANNEL

It was on a summer morning in 1965 that I met Edward Baynes for the first time since our student days in pre-war Oxford.

I was resting, I remember, on a seat in Church Close at Melbridge, waiting for my wife's return from her weekly shopping expedition in East Street, when I saw a big man in clerical dress striding towards me. Recognition was mutual and immediate.

'My dear chap . . . surprise, surprise . . . and I thought I was approaching a lonely stranger . . .'

Here, it is sufficient to say that clerical dress seemed to enhance the man's physical strength, his natural authority and his welcoming smile.

Our former friendship was unfussily renewed. Sometimes we would meet at the church or in the Melbridge Club and, on more festive occasions, at the Feathers! But despite the uncertain intervals between each encounter, our renewed friendship remained firm and was equally dear to both of us.

From time to time, as the vicar of Melbridge, Edward Baynes will appear in the course of this story. But I introduce you to him before it begins, partly because he was the first to inspire my interest in the course of Joe Selby's marriage, but chiefly because his very special position in Melbridge gave him a unique standpoint from which to view the passing scene.

1

People who live in the Southern Counties of England may well have
visited the small town of Melbridge; perhaps to dine at the Three
Feathers which is still managed by the Grant family, or to buy
something special in its East Street shops. But those who live
further afield may like to possess some background material about
the place where the Selby family came to live after the First World
War.

Melbridge, then, is a small town sited on rising ground above the
Mel river. It lies some ten miles south of Melchester and five miles
north of the Mel estuary and Abbotshaven – once the ancient port of
Melchester, but today better known for its yacht basin and the high-
spending mob of weekend sailors whose boats crowd its moorings.

Melbridge, described as Abbot's Melbridge in early chronicles, has
no historic significance though Baedeker once informed his readers
that 'the parish church rates a visit.' But whatever its appeal to
tourists, the church of St Peter and St Paul has its own special
significance in that its position in the centre of Melbridge has dictated
the shape of the town and, to some extent, the nature of its
inhabitants.

Edward Baynes, the present incumbent of St Peter and St Paul,
states in his history of Melbridge that the church owes its existence to
monks from the great Abbey of Melchester who shrewdly built their
daughter church on the high ground above the water-meadows
through which the Mel river flows placidly south towards the sea.
When the agents of Henry VIII plundered the wealth and estates of
the great religious houses such as Melchester Abbey, they spared the
daughter church at Melbridge because it possessed no land of

commercial value. Indeed, this foundation suffered nothing more serious than a change of name in favour of Peter and Paul. It was probably luck, rather than foresight, that allowed the reformed state Church to retain an acre of land surrounding the church. Hence, like a miniature cathedral, the Parish Church of St Peter and St Paul has determined the lay-out of the small township which has sprung up round it. For 450 years, Melbridge has hardly changed its shape except along the south side of the Close where a wealthy eighteenth-century vicar satisfied his craving for fame in this world by erecting a magnificent row of period houses. The best of these he retained for a vicarage for his own large family.

It was back in 1920 that Isaac Selby brought his young wife, Rachel, to Melbridge. Both of them, like their parents and grandparents before them, were members of that fundamentalist Christian sect known as the Plymouth Brethren. They were, therefore, strict teetotallers. They did not smoke, nor did they gamble. The theatre, though not the concert hall, was forbidden ground. On the other hand, their knowledge of the Bible was encyclopaedic. To them its authority was absolute and seemed to be vested in the father as head of the family. Isaac and Rachel Selby accepted these religious restraints without question or complaint: it was the way they had both been brought up. But in the absence of a local Meeting House to minister to their particular Christian persuasion, they were bound to be somewhat cut off from social intercourse. They were not unhappy in their isolation.

Isaac, however, was a man with an eye to the future and was determined to do his own thing. After passing his Law Society exams and working for some years with a leading Melchester solicitor, he saw in Melbridge the opening he sought – a small town with prosperous citizens, old traditions and no professional rivals. In 1920 he rented a small office in a lane behind the Feathers in West Street and set up his new brass plate for all to see:

SELBY and LEADBITTER
Solicitors and Commissioners for Oaths

Leadbitter was a 'surprise number', a fictitious character invented by Isaac because he thought that it made his new brass plate look more impressive. Unlike his wife, he had a very pleasing sense of humour. He laughed aside the criticism of his over-righteous Rachel.

'You, my love, are my only true partner. It is up to you to help me decide on the right shape for Mr Leadbitter. Is he to be a Gideon, or a Daniel or a Gamalial? We shall see, my dear, we shall see.'

Two years later, 'Leadbitter' materialised in the person of Mr Owen Jones, a young man from Melchester who was well qualified to oversee the firm's books and clients' accounts. There was another good reason for selecting Mr Owen Jones. Isaac Selby believed passionately that a solicitor's office should be dust free and tidy. In spite of the cramped conditions of the premises in Feathers Lane, Owen Jones ensured that the offices of Selby & Leadbitter were a model of cleanliness, in marked contrast to the lawyers' offices as pictured by Dickens and too often perpetuated by their successors into the twentieth century.

The early years of the firm were also marked by the birth of a son to Isaac and Rachel Selby. The boy was named Joseph, thus following a family tradition that Selby children should always carry biblical names. To Isaac's grief, Rachel was desperately ill following a difficult birth, and the boy Joseph was to grow up without brothers or sisters. From the day of his birth, he was inevitably designated the heir to his father's legal practice.

The success of the practice was never in doubt. Melbridge people began to bring their problems and Wills into Selby & Leadbitter and became familiar with the neat, authoritative, bearded figure of Mr Isaac Selby walking the streets of Melbridge or riding into town on his bicycle. By the fifties he was widely respected by his fellow citizens as a wise counsellor and as a generous professional man who, in various public offices, had always kept the interests of the town as his first priority.

At first sight, Joseph Selby seemed very like his father. Although clean-shaven, his strong stocky figure, the grey eyes and the sober well-cut suits constantly reminded clients of the old man. There was also, as with his father, a shyness (or was it aloofness?) which discouraged closer friendship. Some people ascribed this characteristic to the strict nature of the Selbys' religious belief, but the grammar school headmaster saw it differently.

'I've had other boys in the school as clever as Joe Selby,' he told his wife, 'but nobody so calculating and so determined to get to the top of the tree. You mark my words. Joe means to be a bigger shot than his father. He is less humble and more personally ambitious: and, in my book, ambition and friendship rarely march hand in hand.'

Certainly in 1957 the people of Melbridge were taken completely by surprise when the staid thirty-four-year-old solicitor, who had previously shown no interest in the ladies of Melbridge, announced his engagement to Kathy Hardingham, the nineteen-year-old eldest daughter of Jack Hardingham, one of the five tenant farmers on Lord Melchester's estate.

The Selby–Hardingham engagement also revived a tenuous link between Melbridge and Lord Melchester's estate office, run by Bob Withers from the west wing of Melchester Court.

The rest of this over-large Victorian mansion, which lies some twelve miles north-west of Melbridge, was occupied in the thirties by the Melchesters and their domestic staff, at the centre of a near-feudal commune, sufficient unto itself alone. A dozen families lived close to the big house and the Home Farm in a scatter of tied cottages which had been modernised after the 1914–18 war. Those who lived there had been pleased to serve the Melchester family inside the house or outside in the fields, according to their individual capacities. Collectively, they included house decorating, plumbing, electrical and mechanical engineering skills among their accomplishments and their families were well supplied with milk, eggs and vegetables from the Home Farm. It was a happy place in which to live.

From time to time a son or daughter would venture into the wider world to seek a partner in marriage, and the children needed to walk three miles to the school in Holmesdale village. But by and large, you could well imagine that this little community was much further from the town of Melbridge than the twelve miles measured by the road map. When the 4th Earl and his wife died in a car accident the title passed to the 4th Earl's brother. But the latter was killed at Alamein, and his son Freddy inherited the title at the age of three.

Inevitably the bond of personal loyalty which had held the Court people together had weakened. Nobody knew whether the 6th Earl – when he came of age – would regard his inheritance as a source of income or a way of life. Shrewd tenant farmers like Jack Hardingham were aware that the old order was changing. Their future might well depend on the willingness and ability of Bob Withers to continue his employment as Freddy Melchester's agent.

2

Kathy's parents, Jack and Liz Hardingham, were not unknown to Melbridge residents, though they lived at Holmesdale village some ten miles from the town. Jack, a highly respected tenant farmer on the Melchester estate worked three hundred acres to the west of the Mel river, living at Buckley's, an eighteenth-century farmhouse which went with the tenancy. Like his father before him, Jack had always enjoyed the old 4th Earl's confidence, dining from time to time at Melchester Court. He had also prospered from the farming boom of the war years.

By 1956 Kathy, the eldest of the four Hardingham children, had emerged from Melchester High School for Girls a happy and successful eighteen-year-old, modestly conscious that she was one of the prettiest girls for miles around. Not that she spent much time in front of a mirror. One tends to underrate one's good looks when a brother and two younger sisters are guaranteed to prick one's pride.

She was best known locally as a useful tennis player who combined determination with a natural ability for the game. But these gifts, as her mother and teachers could testify, hid a character of strong impulse and romantic temperament. In Melbridge and Melchester, many a lad was conscious of Kathy Hardingham – the natural wave of her auburn hair, the trim figure, the humorous sparkling brown eyes and the smile that came easily to her lips. There were many telephone calls to Buckley's Farm, and hopeful young men made innumerable dates.

But Kathy had little use for them. She gave no encouragement to their fumbling hands and crude approaches. She disliked them, as bogus imitations of the love sequences imported from Hollywood and on view each week in Melbridge's only cinema down by the station. She wished the lads would just grow up or be themselves. She was, you might say, a rather fastidious person. Certainly no favourite boyfriend emerged from the pack of admirers, until Kathy joined the voluntary choir which, Sunday by Sunday, enlivened the evening services at the Parish Church. It was here that she first met Isaac Selby's son, Joseph.

The latter was still living at his parents' house – one of a cluster grouped around a small Methodist chapel and burial ground, which lay half a mile beyond Buckley's. So, what more natural than Joseph and Kathy joining each other for the bicycle ride home? And what more charming than Joe's purchase of a new battery for Kathy's bicycle lamp? And what of the steep hill leading up to Holmesdale village? Kathy noted with pleasure the breadth of Joe's shoulders and his co-ordination of muscle as he insisted on pushing both bicycles to the top of the hill. Here was a man who really showed up the boys. And then there was Joe's gallantry when the onset of a summer storm forced the two of them to dismount until the rain stopped. Quick as lightning, Joe pulled a pac-mac out of his saddlebag. 'Here you are, Kathy,' he said, 'there's room for both of us in this ridiculous garment,' and they'd sheltered, literally wrapped together, till the storm passed. Joe had even produced a clean white handkerchief to protect her hair and she had felt his heart beating and his hand caressing her forehead as he adjusted the handkerchief. A momentary tremor of excitement shot through her. She looked up and kissed him very lightly and was sure he held her more tightly.

The moment passed; but after he left her at Buckley's she remembered his courtesy – how calm and gentle he had been in his approach, how much more appealing than the boys of her own generation. It did not take her long to convince her parents that this was the man she was going to marry.

The engagement of a nineteen-year-old girl to a staid solicitor, fifteen years her senior, would be a matter of comment in any small town community, and Melbridge was no exception.

Anybody with long ears would have heard a certain amount of gossip in the Melbridge Club.

'Joe Selby getting hitched up to Jack Hardingham's eldest? A real beauty, too. Cunning old stoat . . . shows what goes on in church, eh?'

But members tended to whisper rather than shout their views. Come to think of it, the Selbys, father and son, were both members of the club. So was Kathy's father, Jack Hardingham, who looked in most Thursdays which was market day in Melbridge. Then, too, the vicar was often in the club – sometimes for a snack lunch, sometimes to play chess with Isaac Selby, sometimes for a game of snooker and a glass of beer with one of his parishioners. In Melbridge Edward Baynes' opinion carried considerable weight and it soon became known that Joe Selby's forthcoming marriage to Kathy Hardingham had the vicar's approval.

In fact, the priest had been in close touch with the Selby family for the past four years, after Joseph had expressed a wish to join the Church of England. It was a situation requiring tact for a man who admired Isaac Selby's sturdy character and that reliance on the Bible wisdom which guided every Plymouth Brother in the conduct of his daily life. Indeed Edward Baynes often asked himself what had been the true motives behind Joe Selby's request. He found it far easier to talk with the father than argue with the prickly Rachel, and was nervous lest he should appear to be trying to undermine the fundamentalist creed which governed every aspect of life in the Selby home. Anyway, it was devilish hard to analyse Joseph's motive. Was it religious conviction or a deliberate act, for instance, to break free of parental control? Or a wish to gain the Hardinghams' acceptance of him as a son-in-law – Jack being vicar's warden at St Wilfred's, Holmesdale and his wife Elizabeth involved in many of the church's social activities? Was Joe influenced by a wish to please young Kathy? Or even – perish the thought – to further his standing in Melbridge and speed the advancement of his legal practice? Only after much diplomatic talk with Isaac and Rachel Selby and probing discussion with their son, did the vicar of Melbridge arrange with the Bishop of Melchester for Joe Selby to be confirmed in the cathedral, well away from the Melbridge small talk. And now, so soon after Joseph's acceptance into the Church of England, came the news of his engagement to Kathy Hardingham. Ted Baynes could only pray that the fifteen-year age gap between bride and bridegroom would not prove too great a hindrance to their future happiness.

Louder and less generous comment came from the ladies of Melbridge – both in the comparative privacy of afternoon bridge parties, and in the more public exposure of Miss Hayward's coffee shop in East Street. Dolly Hayward – sometimes referred to by Melbridgians as 'the lady cakemaker' – was well respected in the local community, having won special marks for her courage in setting up her coffee and cake shop after her paratrooper husband's death at Arnhem. She now lived in a flat above the shop which provided an admirable rendezvous for East Street shoppers and their friends. Park early, shop early, and get a table at the lady cakemaker's not later than ten forty-five a.m. The quality of the cakes and freshly ground coffee – not to mention a wide range of specially blended teas – was matched by Dolly Hayward's prices. But nobody would think of questioning the expense. East Street, after all, was the quality shopping area of the town; and you would be unlucky if you did not encounter a friend at Dolly's establishment and pick up the local gossip.

'Haven't you heard? Haven't you heard? Such a lovely girl, my dear . . . What on earth does she see in that old stick of a solicitor? Her mother's behind it . . . you mark my words . . . A nice social rise for a farmer's daughter, you know, marrying into the law.'

So the gossip continued until a country wedding at St Wilfred's Holmesdale put an end to speculation. In due course, Mr Joseph Selby and young Mrs Selby settled into number 10 Ockenham Drive, one of those new houses just off the Melchester Road; and the ladies of Melbridge turned their attention to other riveting subjects such as Dr Latimer's ill-concealed anger when his wife failed to respond to his bid and he missed out on an odds-on grandslam.

From Edward Baynes' Diary, 1960

The Living of Melbridge has often been a step on the road to higher office and I am considered fortunate to have been offered the appointment when still comparatively young. That I have refused offers of further advancement stems from my friendship with old Isaac Selby whom I came to know early in my ministry. Although he was many years my senior, we found we had much in common.

One day, when we were lunching together at the Melbridge Club, he turned to me with a question – or should I say assertion?

'Why, my dear Ted, do so many men and women wreck their lives by failing to control their personal ambitions?'

'Money, do you say?'

'Well, I know some people marry for money and fight their colleagues to get the highest-paid jobs. In a class-conscious society others impoverish themselves in order to buy a bigger house or educate their children privately. But do they count the cost?'

I left the rhetorical question unanswered and the old man continued.

'Just think what they lose in terms of happiness. Many of my clients would have escaped much family sorrow, had they observed Cardinal Wolsey's injunction to fling away ambition. In the words of the Old Testament prophet, they should not 'despise the day of small things'.

'Consider your own profession, Ted. Can a Man of God ever aspire to a higher calling than that of parish priest, fully committed to Christ's second Great Commandment?'

Old Isaac Selby was very persuasive.

3

During their six months' engagement, Kathy and Joe often discussed the contrasting types of home in which they had spent their childhood.

Kathy was amazed and appalled at the strictness of the Selbys': not because of the Brethren's concentration on prayer and Bible study – the Hardinghams were, after all, regular attendants at Holmesdale Parish Church and the Hardingham children had Bibles at their bedsides – but rather because of the degree of parental authority to which the only Selby child was subject. One story from Joe's childhood stuck in Kathy's mind. Many years later she would recall it was the first time she had heard the name of Mrs Flora Pennington who served in the Selby home, and was the confidante and constant companion of Rachel Selby. Joe, it seems, was playing with the Pennington boy when a stray shot from the latter's catapult beheaded one of old Pennington's chickens. The sly Mrs Pennington told Mrs Selby that Joe had done the deed (which he hadn't) and Rachel told Isaac.

The latter was implacable in judgement. He didn't care who had aimed the stone from the catapult.

'The crime might just as easily have been committed by you.'

Silence.

'And though the catapult may have been owned by young Pennington you did nothing to stop him aiming at the defenceless chicken, did you?'

Silence.

'Right. Go to your bedroom and repent. You will exist on bread and water until you can recite the Ten Commandments to your

15

mother without a single mistake. And don't bother me with this sort of thing again.'

Joe told the story lightheartedly to Kathy, remarking that the form of punishment had biblical authority behind it. And anyway, it taught him never to trust the Pennington boy again. But he also quoted with bitter resentment a later example of his father's dictatorial ways.

Evidently the grammar school headmaster, impressed by Joseph's ability, had wanted to prepare him for an Oxford scholarship; but Isaac had turned down his request with absolute finality.

'I'm sorry to disappoint you, Headmaster, but in my view Oxford is a sheer waste of time, and so is Cambridge. The law will be Joseph's university, as it has been mine: and it will keep him clear of the foul-mouthed sons of the wealthy and the drunken company they favour. The subject is closed.'

Kathy gained the impression that in Joe's mind the bearded Isaac had a God-given right to a patriarchal power which embodied the authority of an old Testament prophet – even of Jehovah himself. And this was strange because Isaac treated his future daughter-in-law with a most pleasing courtesy and unconcealed affection.

'Joe's a very lucky man, m'dear.' He treated her without condescension, as a mature adult with a mind of her own to match her good looks. 'I reckon you and your family will widen his horizons.'

The young girl and the old man really enjoyed each other's company: which is more than you could say for Kathy's relationship with Rachel Selby, who did not hide her disapproval of her son's choice of partner.

'She's not one of us, this slip of a girl who has cast a spell on Joseph. There will be trouble, Flora Pennington, you mark my words.'

Kathy, much helped by her own mother's advice, resolved to see her future mother-in-law as little as possible until after the wedding.

Not for one moment did Kathy's contacts with the Selby parents weaken her resolve to marry Joe Selby. For her, he remained the strong, stable, reliable character on whom her marriage was going to be built. But sometimes, as they talked, she sensed in him a vulnerability which could easily induce a protective element in her love for him. Womanlike, she rather enjoyed the feeling.

Joe's relationship with the Hardinghams was altogether less complex. With Jack in particular, he loved to discuss the hazards of the farming life and the ways in which a lawyer might have a part to play in it. On one occasion, he was able to obtain repossession of a tied cottage from a Welsh shepherd whose idleness had, for too many years, been a pain in the neck to Jack and his farm workers. On another, he managed to placate some vociferous lobby over a right-of-way claim. A genuine friendship developed between lawyer and farmer and soon extended to Bob Withers, the agent to the Melchester estate. Moreover, Joe was happy to rely on Mrs Hardingham to help Kathy equip the new house they had acquired in Ockenham Drive off the Melchester Road. His own mother showed no interest – better leave her out of it.

And so to the wedding day, on a glorious Saturday in early June, 1958. It was a genuine country wedding. No 'posh' clothes hired for the occasion, but 'Sunday best' as each guest understood the term. And the setting was right – the village church of St Wilfred Holmesdale (cruciform, Norman, AD 1140 for those who bought the guide book). On that summer day the little church was alive with flowers and sunshine; the bridegroom looked very handsome with Bob Withers as best man; the bride wore traditional white with a very proud father leading her up the aisle and with her two younger sisters as bridesmaids. The service, conducted by the vicar assisted by Edward Baynes, took its 1662 appointed course; and as Joe and Kathy emerged from the vestry, the joyful noise of Widor's Toccata shook the tie-beams while a peal of bells proclaimed to the Mel Valley that another couple had become man and wife under the blessing of the old English saint.

What a day to remember!

Joseph and Kathy walked from the west door, across the new-mown grass of the churchyard to the lychgate and thence up 'the street' to Buckley's Farm at the far end of the village, with the villagers clapping and cheering and exchanging good-natured chat as village people have always done.

'That Kathy Hardingham's a real beauty. Her mum made the dresses, yer know ... Seems like only yesterday she was running around in pigtails ... clever they say ... reckon that lawyer's a lucky chap.'

Up at Buckley's the guests circulated about the lawns and weedless garden, fortified by Dolly Hayward's catering and Tom Gutteridge's wines and spirits department. Only poor Rachel missed the fun, resting beside a pot of tea inside Dolly's marquee ('I fear the strong light is too much for my eyes'). Finally, old bearded Isaac Selby, setting aside his ginger beer and looking quite splendid in a frock coat and coloured waistcoat (circa 1910) proposed the health of the bride; and away went Mr and Mrs Joseph Selby in Jack Hardingham's Humber for an unknown destination, where bride and bridegroom transferred themselves and their luggage to Kathy's Morris 1000.

Kathy and Joe were away to a great start. On the way to Budleigh they chattered about the guests ('Your father, Joe, really stole the show with that suit of his'), and as the '1000' chugged along, Joe made his wife promise to teach him to drive as soon as they were back at Melbridge. But, after signing at Reception as Mr and Mrs Selby of Melbridge and seeing their luggage into their bedroom facing the sea, Joe became strangely silent.

'What's the worry, my love?'

'Those women, Kathy. Did you see them in that reception room opposite the office, all of them staring at us?'

'Well, that's the way of things at holiday hotels, isn't it?'

'Oh no, this was different; this was speculating . . . whispering (yes, I'm sure of it) . . . about us. "Old man . . . young woman. Some rich city gent no doubt, giving his secretary a fancy weekend. Disgusting I call it."'

'Joe, my dear, you're imagining things.'

'Maybe . . . but I tell you I can't stand the idea of dining in the same room – and hardly any space between the tables.'

'Well then,' Kathy was always practical, 'how about missing out on dinner, taking a stroll through the town, stopping somewhere for a coffee and so to bed, with breakfast in our room in the morning?'

Which is what they did. But once upstairs, Joe became tense and uncommunicative again. Kathy, nervous enough in all conscience, wondered how Joe would proceed, how far he would follow the various approaches suggested in the magazines over which the girls of Melchester High had often giggled in their schooldays.

She would laugh later about her first night of marriage but it was anything but funny at the time: Joe undressing on one side of the room, very slowly arranging his clothes . . . herself reluctantly reaching for the lovely short diaphanous nightie which her sisters had given her and, sensing no help from Joe, slipping into bed ... aware that he'd been watching her ... waiting ... and suddenly Joe sobbing (she'd never heard a man crying before) ... 'Darling, I'm sorry ... I've wanted you so badly ... too excited ... and now ...'

She had understood and comforted him as if he were a child. 'Don't worry, Joe,' she said. 'Don't worry. We've a lifetime ahead of us.'

Joe had fallen asleep in her arms and in the dawn it had all come right and Kathy had thanked God for the down-to-earth biology mistress who had taught the girls of Melchester High objectively and explicitly what sex was all about.

But his fellow guests still worried Joe. Something had to be done and Kathy proposed they leave the hotel and find a place where they could be alone and cater for themselves. In this they were fortunate, for they found a National Trust cottage suddenly empty. Kathy was triumphant.

'At Port Isaac, too, Joe. That's a good biblical name for the Selbys ... must be a sign.' By midday Kathy was driving her little car towards the north Cornwall coast. The troubles of newlyweds behind them, they enjoyed every moment of their holiday, sharing the catering, cooking and housekeeping together; walking and picnicking on the moorland; and enjoying the grandeur and solitude that Cornwall offers, bathing in the cove above which their cottage stood.

It was here that Kathy first discovered that her husband was a superb swimmer.

'Ever heard the Greek story,' he asked her one day, 'about the dolphin who brought the missing boy home to his parents? No? Well, I'll show you. I'm the dolphin and you are the boy, see? Hop on to my back. Off we go.' And with Kathy astride his broad back, Joe brought her swiftly to land.

The following day, Joe's prowess was more seriously tested. He and Kathy were spreading a rug and laying out a picnic after bathing. At the time, there was only one other family sharing the beach – a mother and four small children. The mother was playing with the baby while the other three were fooling about in the water.

Suddenly, Joe saw that the eldest boy, who could swim, was in trouble with a dangerous current driving him further out to sea on the ebb tide.

In a flash, Joe had shed his shirt and was sprinting towards the water. 'Tell the family,' he shouted to Kathy, 'find the old man with the boat, that lad is in real trouble.'

With his powerful crawl, Joe reached the boy just as he was going under, held him firmly in the lifesaving position and headed for the land. It was heroic stuff by any standard, but progress against the current was desperately slow. There could so easily have been 'another drowning tragedy off the Cornish coast' if Kathy had not succeeded in alerting the old fisherman who owned the boat with the outboard motor.

Joe and Kathy returned to Melbridge happy in their love. They had proved to each other that, in their separate ways, they knew how to act in a crisis.

4

Ockenham Drive comprises twenty detached houses, built after the war as a single development under a single master plan. The houses vary between four or five bedrooms and single or double garages, the larger models being placed at the far end of the cul-de-sac and overlooking a pleasant square of mown grass and newly planted flowering trees. The gardens are small and easily managed. In those post-war years such houses could be bought by anybody who could lay hands on £5,000.

The Selbys counted themselves fortunate to have bought one of the four-bedroom double-garage models, which was five houses away from the busy Melchester Road. Number ten was within easy walking distance of the Selby & Leadbitter office in Feathers Lane, and you could reach the East Street shops on foot by crossing Church Close or walking along North Street past the grammar school. The new house offered Kathy two additional advantages. The Melchester bus stopped close to the point where the drive joined the Melchester Road; and the tennis club, where Kathy had played as a schoolgirl and numbered many friends among its members, was less than a mile away.

Shrewd old Isaac Selby agreed that Joseph had done well to buy number ten for £3,500. 'There's no sounder investment than property, my children. According to my reading of history, house values always rise provided you can afford to bide your time.'

For the Selbys those first five years of married life at number ten were joyful years.

In the early days of her marriage Kathy found herself with far more time on her hands than most of her contemporaries who had recently set up new homes in the district, for Joe was working an eight-to-eight, twelve-hour day – and extremely tired when he returned home at night. But she accepted her lot with a good grace, especially after she knew she was pregnant. This was how she and Joe had planned it.

Most of the newlyweds found good reasons for delaying the birth of children: 'There was the mortgage, my dear . . . and the never-never on the dining-room furniture . . . and children do tie you down, don't they?' But Kathy would have none of it. She was an even-tempered girl, but she lost her temper with a friend who implied that she was starting a family at once because of Joe's age.

'Joe's age? What do you mean? I want to have children right away because I like it that way – and so does my husband.'

As for Joe, he was bound to be heavily involved in the day-to-day running of the practice, now that Isaac was growing old and working more slowly. But the workload had been greatly increased by the problems referred to Selby & Leadbitter by the Melchester estate office. This development was of recent growth, stemming from Joe's introduction to Kathy's family, and hence, through Jack Hardingham, to Lord Melchester's agent, Bob Withers.

The latter, the younger son of a county family and a product of Blundell's and Cirencester, was dedicated to the improvement of farm management in England, and an immediate rapport had developed between him and the equally dedicated lawyer. In Dolly Hayward's coffee shop people would have noted with interest that Bob Withers acted as best man at the Selby–Hardingham wedding in Holmesdale. But two years before that well-publicised affair, Bob had asked Joe to deal with a series of minor problems which he felt could be handled more swiftly by a local solicitor than by the Melchester family solicitors in London. He had, indeed, been impressed by the excellence of Joe's advice and the speed with which he had acted.

It seemed natural, therefore, for Bob Withers to discuss with Joe the major problem of the long-delayed bypass round the city of Melchester.

The two men were drinking coffee after a snack lunch at the Feathers in West Street when Bob Withers raised the subject.

'You know, Joe, that the planning people will soon be holding a final meeting to decide the route for the Melchester bypass?'

'Of course I do. But it's a simple problem, isn't it, now that everybody is screaming to get it started and finished? Or, at least, the problem is reduced to a simple question: is it to run north or south of the city?'

Withers laughed. 'Simple? My God, you should see the reams of paper proposing, rejecting, amending, arguing . . . in my office, you can't see the view for the paper . . .'

'Just keep the problem simple, Bob. Is the road to run north or south of the city? Your master has the key in his pocket.'

'How do you mean?'

'Well, look at the map. If the bypass runs north, the planners will need to satisfy a host of property owners, small-holders, and a few strongly established industries. But south? The road could run entirely through His Lordship's land, crossing the Mel river midway between Melbridge and Melchester.'

'Split the estate in two, eh?'

'Put it that way, if you like. But I wouldn't be surprised to learn that His Lordship is interested in cashing some of his fixed assets. I reckon he could secure at least £30,000 in compensation, and insist on at least two bridges to connect the southern part of his land with the acres on the northern, or Melchester side, of the bypass.'

'You think cash compensation could reach as much as £30,000?' Withers was well aware that young Melchester had expensive tastes.

'Thirty thousand, you know, would only be the start of the cash flow. For example, I hear that influential people in Melchester are crying out for a new eighteen-hole golf course . . . new golf courses are sometimes surrounded by high-quality houses . . . they could be very attractive to boss men in Melchester . . . only ten miles from the city, you know.'

'Good Heavens, Joe. How long have you been working on this one?'

Joe Selby smiled. 'You could say, Bob, that I have a speculative mind, but His Lordship will naturally consult his own advisers. My guess, for what it's worth, is that if the commissioners know in advance that Lord Melchester favours the southern route, the matter will be quickly settled.'

'And what of the outgoings . . . the cost of legal representation and all that?'

23

'Again, I think you must consult His Lordship's advisers. I can only claim that I know the law and the locality. Personally, I believe you can win the case without the help of Learned Council. Anyway, it's worth a thought.'

Joe Selby walked home through the Close that evening, well satisfied with the effect of his lunchtime talk on Bob Withers. He greeted Kathy with unusual affection. What a joy to know that he could safely leave the household cares of number ten to his capable young bride. He may have been grateful, too, though he might never admit it, that under her tutelage his early inhibitions had disappeared so that there was no restraint in their loving.

In May 1959, at the Melbridge Cottage Hospital where twenty-one years before she had first seen the light of day, Kathy gave birth to a daughter who was to be named Rebecca – or Becky for short.

You cannot live long in Melbridge without hearing about this small sixty-bed hospital. It owes its foundation to a most generous bequest from an old unmarried doctor who had once headed the practice now run as a partnership under Dr Latimer's leadership. But the old doctor had made his gift contingent on matching generosity from his fellow citizens. Thus, two of the five wards carried the names of Gutteridge and Collington whose successors still traded in East Street as grocers and drapers. A children's ward had been subscribed by the people of Abbotshaven, while the Friends of Melbridge Hospital attracted strong support from a high percentage of Melbridge residents.

And, in the fifties and sixties, it boasted other unusual features. For instance, the five ward sisters and the staff nurses under them lived in flats adjoining the hospital gardens. Again, local doctors were 'appointed' to the staff without extra pay and were responsible for their own patients once they had been admitted to the hospital. Although surgery was limited to everyday operations – brain and heart surgery being handled by Melchester General – specialists and consultants were always available.

This small and singularly happy hospital owed much of its character to its matron, Matilda Broadbent. Known as Mattie to three generations of Melbridgians, she took special pride in the babies whom, year after year, she helped to bring into the world. Among

24

them had been the four Hardingham children, and Matron was happy to inform young Mrs Selby that she and her baby daughter looked exactly alike at birth.

Two years later, it was Mattie who carried Becky into her mother's light, flower-filled room to take a first look at her baby brother. Following the biblical name tradition of the Selby family the little boy was christened Daniel.

Joe watched the development of his two children with obvious delight, but happy to leave their care and education in Kathy's hands. Was he, Kathy wondered, deliberately distancing himself from the Selby tradition of paternal authority he'd known in his old home? Or did he delegate so much to her only because the legal practice was keeping him so busy?

It was while they were enjoying a family holiday in the familiar surroundings of Port Isaac ('Grampa's private harbour', Becky had told her brother) that Joe raised with his wife the inevitable question of birth control.

'Contraception?'

'Yes, Kathy, I understand. We've agreed to limit ourselves to two children, and so . . . but Kathy darling . . .'

'What's the worry, Joe? Having second thoughts?'

'No, no, of course not, but I don't like all those newspaper articles about the Pill. Latimer talks about the need for further tests and possible side effects . . . and I don't want you involving yourself in all those other contraptions . . .'

'Well really, Joe. If that's how you feel, you'll have to fix yourself . . .'

'Yes, darling. But can you possibly arrange things for me? You know what I mean . . . small town . . . people talking . . .'

Kathy wanted to burst out laughing. On intimate occasions such as this she sometimes wondered whether she had not chosen for a husband a survivor from another age. And then she remembered the happiness of the past five years. She might have taught him a thing or two, but – bless him – he'd shown himself an excellent pupil. And did not her friends have their problems too? She wouldn't want to be Gwenda whose Rugby-playing husband came home tanked-up every Saturday night. Or Betty Lindhurst, embarrassed by the financial problems of a charming but incompetent husband who seemed unable to hold down a job for more than six months at a time. She'd prefer to cope with her own man's minor inhibitions – and count herself lucky.

Somehow, she managed to control her laughter and her temper.

'No trouble at all, Joe,' she assured him, as if she was being asked to buy a bottle of cough mixture. 'I'll pop into the chemist's in the morning.'

Kathy was never short of friends, and the children led to new friendships – first at the twice-weekly crêche for small children held in the church rooms on Southside, and later at meeting points like the playgroup and the Church of England primary school with other parents who were waiting to collect their children.

The crêche, organised by Mrs Baynes and volunteers from the parish church, was especially welcome to the young mothers of Melbridge. Twice a week, on Tuesdays and Thursdays, you could deposit your children in good hands and do your shopping in East Street, unencumbered by prams or the importunate clamour of children. It afforded you time, if you so wished, to pause for a coffee at Dolly Hayward's or do a little window shopping at Collington's, the drapers, or study the latest fashions at the newly opened Marcelle de Paris.

And, finally, there was the walk home across Church Close – no traffic to worry about, and the likelihood of encountering other Melbridge characters, like Harold Leng the organist at St Peter and St Paul, or Edward Baynes.

On a fine day, the latter's progress from the church to his vicarage was anything but straightforward. If he saw somebody sitting alone on one of the seats in the Close he would stop to 'pass the time of day'. More often, he would be assailed by children racing ahead of mothers laden with the week's shopping. He was naturally approachable – a fine-looking man in early middle age with the spring of an athlete in his step and only a hint of the scholar in his features. In Melbridge he was immediately identified by his clerical habit (none of those trendy 'one of the boys' old flannel trousers and high-necked pullovers for Mr Baynes or his curates): but his insistence on being correctly dressed did not make him less approachable. No man in Melbridge was better known or more widely trusted. The children especially liked him because he treated them as if they were adults. He never spoke down to the children. They enjoyed the same rights of membership as their parents and grandparents in the parish over which Edward Baynes presided.

5

While the children were young the Selby family always spent their summer holidays at Port Isaac. Children seem to prefer the familiarity of the places they know, and Becky and Daniel had grown to love the rocks and inlets of the Cornish coast. They had walked the high moors and crossed the coombes and discovered and re-discovered special spots for picnics. They knew the local shopkeepers of the little town, and fishermen like the old man who owned the boat with the outboard motor at Port Gaverne. It was he who had taught both children to swim.

'Not like one o' them fancy professors at the big city swimming baths,' he'd say, 'but yer learn quickest when ye're chucked into deep seawater from my liddle boat . . . an' there's yer dad bobbin' about in the water to show yer 'ow easy it is. Yes, yer'll need to walk a long way before yer'd find a stronger swimmer then your dad.'

The old fisherman spoke truer than he knew. For Becky and Daniel (and, indeed, for Kathy too), one of the joys of those Cornish holidays was that Dad was always 'bobbin' around' – and not only while they were bathing. It was Dad who read the maps and discovered the most exciting places to visit. It was Dad who told them of the quarrel between Uther Pendragon and the Duke of Cornwall as the family climbed the spectacular rock of Tintagel, three hundred feet above the Atlantic breakers; and Dad again, who peopled mysterious Camelot with romantic knights and ladies. When Becky, who had read her Tennyson, asked him who King Arthur really was, he told her it was a question that had often been asked but never fully answered.

'But, Dad, who do *you* think he was?'

'Well, my dear, I doubt if Tennyson's idylls tell the true story. His heroes and heroines seem to me to have popped out of a Victorian drawing-room for a game of croquet on a weedless lawn.' He laughed. 'No, I should not spoil the poet's picture, but, as you ask me, I reckon that King Arthur was a very brave soldier and a great leader – probably a Roman – who conducted a magnificent defensive action against overwhelming forces, retreating across the South of England with such skill that in the end his enemies, the Saxon invaders, gave up the chase. That would perhaps explain why Cornish folk who came west with Arthur seem so different from the English.'

Joe Selby was, indeed, part of the holiday scene, so that the children were thoroughly upset when, in 1972, he announced that, because of the pressure of business, he could not join them at Port Isaac. Becky and Daniel appealed to Kathy.

'Come on, Mum. Can't you persuade Dad to leave Grandpa in charge of that silly old office? Holidays won't be the same without Dad.'

But Joe was adamant and Kathy was left to seek a compromise by letting each child invite a school friend to share the holiday with them.

In the event, the children thoroughly enjoyed their holiday, but it was soon forgotten in the excitement of their mother's success in the Melchester Open Tennis Tournament, which was crowned by a *Melchester Chronicle* picture headed, 'Melbridge couple embrace after surprise win'.

To be fair to the editor this surprise really was headline local news. For many years the city's tennis club had staged an open tournament in the second week of September – the last of a chain of similar tournaments run by similar clubs in the South of England. Each year they attracted players of considerable quality, but just short of Wimbledon class. Attracted by a high standard of local hospitality and handsome prizes, these 'mini-stars' looked on this series of tournaments as an enjoyable holiday in which they would meet old friends and make new ones. The task of the better local players was to provide the opposition with cannon-fodder, so to speak, to be used up and removed in the early rounds of each event. But the elimination of a touring 'mini-star' always remained a glorious possibility. Hence there was much excitement when Kathy teamed up

30

with a young Melbridge doctor to win the Open Mixed Doubles Challenge Bowl at Melchester.

Oliver Carstairs had only recently joined Dr Latimer's practice after gaining a tennis blue at Oxford and qualifying at Guy's. As a good-looking and unattached bachelor, he naturally aroused considerable speculation among those who met for elevenses at Dolly Hayward's in East Street.

Entering the Melchester Open Tournament with Kathy Selby had followed from a casual meeting at the local tennis club where she had easily regained her place in the 'first six' after Becky and Daniel were off her hands. What was totally surprising was their round-by-round success until they achieved final victory in the Open Mixed Doubles. It had never been done before.

At Buckley's Jack and Liz Hardingham hosted a celebratory dinner which, in addition to Kathy and Oliver Carstairs, included Joe Selby and his father, Bob Withers, the Hardingham children and Matilda Broadbent. With Rachel staying away ('My migraine, Isaac, you must excuse me'), joy was unconfined. Joe appeared immensely proud of his wife's success, and so did her father-in-law (but as Matty Broadbent once told him, 'Isaac, you've been potty about that girl from the day you first met her').

Elsewhere in Melbridge, there was a rather more mixed reception to the news, and especially to the *Chronicle* front page photograph which showed Kathy hugging the young doctor at their moment of victory.

'What a sauce ... very embarrassing, my dear, for young Dr Carstairs ... and Dr Latimer too, I shouldn't wonder ... nonsense, Angela ... Anyway, he is hugging her ... And why not, for Heaven's sake? Well, you stick to your opinion and I'll stick to mine ...' The duellists paid their bills and parted company, with the sourpuss getting in a final thrust: 'And how do you think Joseph Selby will be feeling about his wife's new partner?'

But the most bitter comments came, as you would expect, from the Selby home beside the Methodist church beyond Holmesdale village. Inevitably Flora Pennington had found a copy of the *Chronicle*. She pushed it into Rachel's hands.

'There you are, Rachel. Disgraceful, isn't it? What did I tell you? Joe ought never to have married this young gadabout. Joe did wrong.

I've said it before and I'll say it again. No good will come of that marriage. As the good book tells us, "there is no peace for the wicked."'

Nobody in the family took the two women seriously any more. It seemed as if Isaac had transferred his first love for Rachel into a latterday love for his daughter-in-law. In his eyes, Kathy could do no wrong.

She continued to visit her mother-in-law at regular intervals and kept her informed about the children's progress. But once, in Danny's presence, she unguardedly spoke of Rachel as 'the Witch of Endor' and the boy roared with laughter.

'But Mum, there are two of them up there. Why not call them collectively "the Cows of Bashan"? It's in "the good book", you know, straight from Amos who is one of Grandma Selby's favourite prophets.'

By the end of September the children were back at school – Becky transferred to Melchester High School for Girls as a weekly boarder and Danny moving into the senior section of Melbridge Grammar School – and in the first week of October Kathy found herself driving her husband to Melchester for the final day of the Melchester Bypass Court of Inquiry. Though Joe had passed his driving test in the spring following their marriage, there were occasions, such as today, when he was glad of his wife's presence at the wheel while he marshalled his mental resources for the day ahead.

Kathy glanced at her companion sitting silent in the passenger seat of the Morris. Smartly dressed in clerical grey and wearing the dark red tie she had given him at Christmas, Joe looked totally relaxed and ready for his great day. Kathy was far too wise to distract him with family chatter.

Her mind returned to private speculation about the children's future.

Becky was changing naturally and easily from a bouncy, smiling child into a thinking adolescent. She exhibited a special interest in the sciences and would have no trouble with her 'O'-levels. Suitably encouraged, she might move on to get professional qualifications.

Danny was altogether more complicated. Bespectacled and rather small for his age, he managed to remain in the top half of his form without any apparent effort. Because of a certain histrionic gift, he was regarded by schoolmates and school staff as something of a 'character'. But there was another side to Danny. From a very early age he had shown an exceptional interest in all things musical. Kathy, who would modestly refer to herself as a hymn-playing pianist, well remembered the four-year-old Danny listening intently to her version of 'Baa Baa Black Sheep'.

'Again, again,' he'd shouted, and a few minutes later, she heard a searching, one-finger repeat performance reaching her in the kitchen.

That was only the start. At eight, he joined the parish church choir. Three years later, he was choir leader with a God-given purity of tone and surety of pitch. At school he took conventional piano lessons, but without any help from his teachers he could harmonise and play by ear any tune that took his or his schoolmates' fancy. His playing – classical or music hall – was only limited by the stretch of his hands.

This led him to agitate for violin lessons, and the organist at St Peter and St Paul's, who was also Head of Music at the grammar school, arranged for him to have lessons after school from a Polish Professor of Music who lived in an enclave of Polish ex-patriates at Abbotshaven. Jan Podolski was staggered by the boy's progress and soon he was joining in string quartets with Jan and his fellow exiles.

Danny's talents were quickly recognised, not only by the Polish community at Abbotshaven, but also by John Lucas, the new headmaster of Melbridge Grammar School, Edward Baynes and his organist Harold Leng. In a town the size of Melbridge you cannot hide so bright a light under a bushel. For Kathy and Joe Selby, equally aware of their son's natural gifts, Danny presented an exciting but somewhat alarming prospect. Whatever hopes might be entertained by Isaac and Joe Selby, it was pellucidly clear to Kathy that Danny was unlikely to become a third-generation partner in Selby & Leadbitter. It was hard to believe that Danny's future would conform to the conventional patterns of life, as understood by the people of Melbridge.

Kathy shut her mind to further speculation as the car approached Melchester and Joe came to life.

'Look, you can park for free at the City Hall. There's a space reserved for the bigwigs though they've left their headgear in

33

London; so today, I shall be one of the nobs.'

He laughed as he kissed his wife goodbye.

'Here's your ticket for a reserved seat in the public gallery, if you really want to see me in action.'

'But of course I do.'

'Well, then, get back here by eleven when the Selby show is due to start. And don't wait to the end of the day. I'm sure Bob Withers will drive me back to number ten.'

'Good luck,' she said and kissed him again. Nobody, she knew, was better prepared and nobody would look more handsome in court than Mr Joseph Selby of Melbridge.

As she took her seat beside Bob Withers in the public gallery, she recognised Joe's voice, unhurried, musical, persuasive, patient and spotted him standing in the body of the hall. He was addressing a middle-aged, good-looking man from the Ministry of Transport who was presiding over a gaggle of scribbling clerks and listening lawyers. They looked, thought Kathy, as if they were more than ready for the luncheon break; but an occasional flutter showed that they were sleepily alert to their particular interests, ranging from the Department of Transport and the County Council to private householders, public companies and the North Melchester Housing Association.

With a quick look at his watch, Joseph came to the point.

'My submission, sir, can be briefly stated. As the court is aware, my client holds the freehold of the arable land which has to be crossed should the Ministry decide to adopt the southern route for the Melchester bypass. I am happy to confirm that the Melchester Estate Office will offer no objection to such a course.'

Suddenly the peace of the Inquiry was shattered by the shouts of a shoddily dressed fellow with an open shirt, a red face and wildly waving hair.

''Alf a mo', mister. Will you be so good as to tell the court 'ow many grand 'is Lordship aims to make out of this little transaction? I'm a Melchester citizen and I've a right to know . . .'

Joe immediately resumed his seat with an inquiring look to the president – as much as to say, 'Would you prefer to field this one?'

The red-faced fellow never got beyond his 'rights' before the president quickly called Mr Sopwith QC, representing the City of

Melchester, to explain to the gentleman outside the court that this Inquiry was concerned with the route of the Melchester bypass, and not the cash compensation of those affected by it.

'Yes, outside the court, if you please, Mr Sopwith.'

The red-faced fellow was led from the court shouting obscenities about this bloody police state, and Joe resumed.

'May I therefore emphasise that, in recommending the southern route, my client is solely actuated by the belief that the southern route will best serve the interests of the people of Melchester for whom the bypass is a crying and urgent necessity.

'We can confirm that the southern route, proposed by the Minister, will not involve the relocation of any residents and the tenant farmers raise no objection to the scheme, provided that the two bridges proposed by the Ministry are strong and wide enough to carry modern farm machinery. (Their signed document of consent, sir, is already lodged with the court.)

'I shall be happy to answer any questions on which this court desires further enlightenment, and Mr Robert Withers, the agent for Melchester Estates Ltd, is present in court should further assurance be needed.

'But perhaps I should make a point concerning the conservation issue. Here the policy of Melchester Estates is crystal clear. All authorised footpaths and rides are carefully preserved; tree planting is a year-on-year activity, to the benefit of birdlife as well as to nature lovers; and hedges are maintained so that in spring the hedgerows are alight with flowers. As to the poisonous fumes emitted by the passing traffic, I feel sure this court will agree that the noise and unhealthy emissions of car exhausts can be absorbed more effectively by open air than by the lungs of North Melchester citizens. And of course there is no possibility that the southern route, which runs seven miles south of the city and well to the north of Melbridge and Holmesdale village, will be used as a service road for manufacturing industry.'

At this point, the court adjourned for lunch and Bob Withers turned to Kathy to congratulate her on Joe's performance.

'Very deft, I thought, in handling Red Alec – he's a well-known troublemaker in the city, you know; and remarkably suave in pre-empting the conservationists who always sing a song of protest at these Inquiries. Let's go and join Joe, shall we, for a quick snack?'

35

Inevitably, the *Melchester Chronicle*'s report on the court proceedings gave Red Alec's performance a 'Row in Court' headline. But, to the delight of many friends in Melbridge, the *Chronicle* also included a charming picture of the scene outside the City Hall: 'Mrs Selby wishes good luck to her husband, the Melbridge solicitor who represents Lord Melchester and the Melchester Estate Office at the Bypass Court of Inquiry.'

6

Two years later, the name of Selby was once again the talk of Melbridge – on this occasion through Danny Selby's participation in a concert organised by the headmaster of Melbridge Grammar School.

This was to be no ordinary school concert. John Lucas, supported by his Governing Body, was determined that his school should retain its independent status, for which purpose he wanted to enlist the total backing of people living in Melbridge, Abbotshaven and the surrounding villages. How better to win public support than by sponsoring a concert and getting the whole of Melbridge involved? Inspiration came to him through the old Polish violinist from Abbotshaven who had been teaching Daniel Selby.

A planning committee was formed, with the headmaster as chairman, Edward Baynes and Dr Latimer representing Melbridge interests, and Professor Podolski and Harry Leng charged to devise a suitable musical programme. Having agreed that tickets should be sold at £3.00 each and all receipts given to Melbridge Cottage Hospital for the purchase of new X-ray equipment, the laymen on the committee handed over the detailed planning to the headmaster's musical advisers.

At this point, Jan Podolski assumed control.

'Permission, please, Headmaster, to give lead. I propose we show Melbridge how splendidly boys make music, what happiness it give them and their fathers, mothers, friends . . . You agree?'

John Lucas nodded.

'OK, very good. But, Mr Lucas, we also show how simple is music . . . international language, yes? Give boys girls instruments at young age – you understand?'

'And can we hear, Professor, exactly how you achieve your purpose in this concert?' The headmaster had no time to spare.

'Right, Mr Lucas and gentlemen. We open concert with rousing chorus, all boys singing . . . a little help maybe from Peter-Paul volunteer choir.' The Professor looked hopefully at Harry Leng. 'I think Verdi very popular today. So we choose Verdi chorus – *Nabucco*, Prisoners' Song perhaps and *Trovatore* "Anvil" and Soldiers' Chorus – good noise, understand, but good tune, also.

'So then,' Podolski paused for breath, 'for central piece I propose Podolski–Selby Interlude . . . with selection piano, violin, maybe vocal . . . to last thirty minutes, no second longer.'

'You mean you team up with young Selby, Professor?'

'But of course, Mr Lucas. Boy very gifted . . . great credit to school . . . no nerves neither . . .' Jan Podolski's imagination was now at full throttle. 'Maybe, who knows? First public appearance of world-famous virtuoso. Remember Menuhin – only ten years old at start career? Danny nearly thirteen . . . and what of Mozart, eh?'

The Professor permitted himself the ghost of a smile. 'And now . . . now I go practise with Danny and coach boys. You, Mr Lucas, you organise back-up please. Compel boys, parents, help with publicity . . . persuade Reverend Baynes to grant use of Peter-Paul church – school assembly room far too small; and why not loudspeakers outside in Close?' The Professor stopped for want of breath, not ideas.

'Wait a moment, Podolski. Aren't you going too far, too fast?'

'No, no, sir. You get church from Mr Baynes. Your science man and his students responsible for all sound equipment. Someone, maybe East Street shops or Melbridge Club or Matilda at hospital show posters, sell tickets . . . yes, and get printer to give programmes free.'

John Lucas intervened to ask about an orchestra, but the Pole was ready with an answer for that too.

'Ah, very good point, Mr Lucas, but already taken to mind.' The Professor tapped his forehead knowingly. 'Polish colleagues at Abbotshaven guarantee provide orchestra – three violin, one 'cello – and Mr Harry Leng play harmonium to give a little depth of sound to Polish strings.'

The Professor, totally carried away, beamed on the committee members.

One of them asked, 'And what, Professor, follows your so-called Podolski–Selby interlude?'

'No problem, sir, no problem at all. We make audience sing ... shout themselves silly, as people say sometime. Let it be Parry's "Jerusalem" ... serves purpose well. But please, sir, may poet's words be included in programme? For some of my friends in Abbotshaven, poet's words have deeper meaning than Parry's music.'

John Lucas freely admitted later that this final request, added to Podolski's bubbling enthusiasm, swept away all his fears and objections. 'We'll show our little world,' he said to himself, 'what Melbridge Grammar School can do.'

For the Selby family at number ten, already thrilled by the part that Danny was billed to play, there was only one snag. The date chosen for the concert, a Friday night in October when the moon would be full, clashed with a vital appointment in London to which Joe Selby was already committed. He was, in fact, due to finalise the salary and conditions of employment for a qualified solicitor whom Isaac and he required most urgently at Selby & Leadbitter. It would be folly to alter the date of the Law Society meeting. But Joe reassured Danny that the London–Melchester train would get him back in time for the concert. In case the train was delayed, he would bag a seat at the back of the church so as to avoid any upheaval in the front seats which the rest of the family would occupy.

In every other respect, all went according to plan. The East Street traders and their friends sold one thousand tickets eight days before the moon was full, so that the nave of the parish church, luckily unencumbered by fixed pews, would be full to capacity. A local builder had agreed to erect a stage between chancel and nave. The vicar had permitted extra chairs in the chancel behind the stage – these to be sold at half price.

The stage was carpeted by Higgins and draped by the Collington family, and a grand piano and harmonium heaved and pushed into place. Even mean old Forshaw, with his printer's sited between the market and the defunct railway station, had been persuaded to run off posters and programmes free of charge. The new radio and television shop in East Street was co-operating with the school in wiring up for outside loudspeakers and it was made known that those without tickets were welcome to bring rugs and chairs into the Close. The programme sellers, recruited from the school, would be instructed to accept any money that freewheelers in the Close liked to give to the hospital. Mrs Grant at the Feathers was arranging for post-concert dinners – with all profits to the hospital. It is truly amazing what can be achieved by a small homogenous township when it turns its heart and mind to a specific purpose.

Backstage, away from these multiple activities, Jan Podolski was directing the performers with all the panache of the famous Polish Lancers whose name he shared. He would himself conduct the boys for the Verdi choruses while Harry Leng completed the orchestration for the Polish strings and the harmonium accompaniment.

The old man was a real perfectionist. Apart from rehearsing the two pieces that he and Danny would play together, he worked hard to get his pupil's German accent right for the Schubert lied with which he planned to conclude the Podolski–Selby interlude.

'Must sing in German, Danny – music demands it, and you, Danny, you will be Franz Schubert singing his own song. Simple tune – you learn piano and song by heart, *nicht wahr*? And remember, Danny, you sing to audience, not to piano.'

'Like Liberace, eh?'

'Oh, my God, *no*. Candlesticks *are forbidden*! You are–' he was lost for a word – 'you are terrible bad Philistine boy.' Clearly, teacher and pupil had a good rapport.

'One final point, Danny. Like all good showmen, you have encore ready. Let it be the Adagio from the Pathétique Sonata. You play it perfect. But no word to nobody, eh?' The Professor put a conspiratorial finger to his lips.

On the big night, blessed by a clear sky, a full moon and no wind to disturb the trees in the Close, the programme was just as Podolski had planned it.

At seven thirty, with the audience expectant and old Isaac Selby and Matilda Broadbent sitting up front with the Selby and Hardingham families, John Lucas made a brief speech of welcome and thanks. Then he handed over control to Podolski.

Fifty boys clambered on to the stage, jostling each other into place. The Polish strings tuned their instruments. Harry Leng took his place at the harmonium, and Jan Podolski, his grizzled face and stubbly grey hair seeming to emphasise his authority, mounted the conductor's podium. The boys were away to a splendid start – the grief of the prisoners and the excitement of the Spanish guerilla bands excellently interpreted.

The stage emptied and Podolski addressed the audience.

'Ladies, gentlemen. All have programmes, yes?' He scanned the packed church.

'Then, no more speech-making. A boy from the school and I make music for you. Enjoy it please. I say no more but to thank my young friend for starting performance with Chopin who is for my nation great musical hero.'

Podolski, a figure of commanding dignity, walked slowly to a chair on the left of the stage, and Danny appeared from the wings. He was casually dressed – dark trousers and white open-necked shirt, his curly hair under control, his spectacles prominent. He moved to the piano seemingly unaware of the audience as he adjusted the piano stool and stretched his fingers. Then suddenly he was off the mark, the rhythm of the waltz taking over, the technique and touch exact. Kathy, sitting between old Isaac Selby and Becky was amazed at her son's performance. You could not doubt the triumph of his debut. Within four minutes, the boy had captured his audience. The applause was acknowledged by a short formal bow, and, with no time wasted, the Professor was at the piano and Danny had taken up his violin. Together they played the Andantino from Mozart's Sonata in B Flat Major – surely some of the happiest music the young Mozart ever composed. Then, with the 'orchestra' giving background support, the Professor and his pupil played the Largo from Bach's Double Violin Concerto. It must be the climax of the Interlude, you might think: a great feat for the players, especially with such a scratch orchestra in support. But there was magic in the air that night. Some inner voice must have whispered to Jan Podolski that Bach would be the wrong note on which to end the Interlude. With a dramatic gesture to the audience, the Professor retired to his chair at the side of the stage and the boy was back at the piano. He waited until there was complete silence through the great church. Then, very softly, he played the opening bars of Schubert's song and turned towards the audience. His pure treble voice, so often heard in the church of St Peter and St Paul, took over from his hands. '*Der Kleine Nussbaum*' lasted for only four minutes but as the last notes of the piano died away, the audience was already clapping and shouting, 'Encore.'

The Professor and the boy bowed and bowed again, but there was no holding the audience. With a charming smile of resignation, Podolski gestured to the boy and went back to the side of the stage once again.

Danny went through the same routine as in the opening Chopin Waltz – checking the seat, quietly exercising his fingers, waiting for the dramatic silence that only he and his piano could shatter. But how different from the charming rhythm of the Chopin. In his selected encore, the Adagio from Beethoven's Pathétique Sonata, he seemed to challenge the happiness of his Melbridge audience with the grief that comes to every man as he lives his earthly life. It was a boy's interpretation of music in which the genius of Beethoven had plumbed the depths of human grief and discovered that love and compassion provide the only answer to tears.

Who shall say whose heart was moved in the parish church of Melbridge that October night? All one can confirm is that Danny's mother found it impossible to control her tears. Old Isaac, sitting beside her, held her hand and whispered, 'Kathy, my darling child, don't apologise for crying. The world would be a poor place if we never let tears speak for us. Come, we'll slip away to number ten, shall we? I'll tell Becky that you're taking me home so that I can avoid the crowds. Becky and her friends will find Joseph and Danny after the show. Don't worry about them.'

And so, Kathy escaped through the north door of the church while the Professor and the audience were preparing to build a new Jerusalem *fortissimo*. Outside, in the cold light of the moon they passed unnoticed through the singing crowd, but as they emerged into North Street they caught up with a small solitary figure, his face white, his head slightly bent as if unsure where his feet were leading him.

'Danny, my darling,' Kathy put her arm round the boy, 'you were really wonderful . . . We are so proud of you.'

'So Dad was there, was he?'

42

'Of course, Danny.' The boy seemed relieved and held his mother more closely.

'Oh, I'm so pleased we've found you,' Kathy continued, 'a bit of luck really. Grandpa and I came away early to avoid the crowd. Oh, I'm so glad.' Kathy babbled on inconsequentially until she had unlocked the front door of number ten.

'Grandpa,' said the boy, 'would you mind awfully if I went straight to bed? I don't know why but I'm feeling rather tired.'

Kathy followed Danny upstairs and sat beside his bed while he munched a Digestive biscuit and drank a mug of hot chocolate. Colour came back to his cheeks as he took off his spectacles and snuggled down the bed. Kathy asked a final question as she kissed him goodnight.

'Were you worried about Dad or something when you were playing the encore?'

'No, Mum, not really. But when I looked at the audience before sitting down at the piano, I could only see you and Grandpa, and I found I was playing the Adagio specially for Grandpa – as if it was my last chance to play for him.' Danny's eyes closed. He was fast asleep before Kathy turned off the light and tiptoed from the room.

Half an hour later, number ten was buzzing with uncomplicated life. Becky and her friends had quickly found her father talking outside the vestry with Jan Podolski. It was from the Professor that Joe learned that Danny had already gone home. The Professor was jubilant.

'Very happy with performance, sir, but Danny would not wait for final curtain. Very exhausted you see after Adagio. Same with many great artists when music speaks to heart as well as mind. Not to worry, sir. Danny will sleep well tonight.'

So Joe returned home with Becky and her friends to find his father had already left for Holmesdale village, driven there by Owen 'Leadbitter' Jones. While the girls of Melchester High remained in the kitchen chattering their way through their particular fry-ups Joseph was at last able to be alone with Kathy in the quiet of the sitting-room. The London train had indeed been running late and he had only just reached his seat in time to see Danny move towards the piano for the opening Chopin. But what a performance! He had been amazed at their son's success.

'It took me right out of this world,' he said, 'he seemed equally at home with piano and violin: and his playing was beautiful. But you know, Kathy, it was his change of mood that amazed me most. When the audience rose to applaud him after that staggering encore I began to wonder which of all these Daniel Selbys was our son. I wonder where on earth his future lies.'

'The future, Joe? It's a long way from the present,' said Kathy. 'And at present, our Danny is fast asleep. When he wakes up tomorrow morning I bet we find the same old Danny coming down late for Saturday breakfast. But tell me, what about your trip to London?'

'Well, I only hope Father will approve my choice. The man I've selected is Richard Fagg age thirty-five, unattached, lots of experience, happy to take on our court work, satisfied with our salary proposals and anxious to get away from London. Yes, I hope he'll meet our needs for the next fifteen years.'

He looked across to Kathy. She was as tired as he was. He doubted how far she would remember Richard Fagg's qualifications next morning.

'Time for bed,' he said. 'I reckon, my darling, we've both had a very busy day.'

7

The attitudes and actions of many people in the town were affected by the success of the Melbridge Grammar School concert. John Lucas and his staff basked in the aura of success – knowing they had conducted a very effective piece of public relations. The Professor found many excuses for visiting Melbridge – sometimes lunching at the Melbridge Club with Harry Leng, sometimes slipping in for a snack at the Feathers. The tall impresario with the stubbly grey hair began to look more and more like the officer commanding the Podolski Lancers. The only character totally unaffected by success seemed to be Daniel Selby for whom tomorrow was just another school day.

On the other hand, his performance deeply influenced members of the family. Kathy and Joe began to worry about his future education, while his grandfather took the bus to Melchester and added a codicil to his Will, duly witnessed at the legal firm for whom he had once worked.

At Melbridge the lovely autumn weather of 1974 continued into November – the winds light, the temperature mild but with a hint of autumn in the air, and the sun shining out of a cloudless blue sky.

Driven into Melbridge by Owen Jones, Isaac Selby still reached his office in Feathers Lane at eight forty-five a.m. each day, but for a year or two had been working a 'mornings only' day. At midday, he would clear up his office and break for lunch – sometimes to take a quick snack with Edward Baynes at the Melbridge Club in Southside, sometimes to visit Matilda Broadbent at the hospital of which he was a governor, sometimes to walk through the Close to number ten and be entertained by Kathy. He could rely on her to take him home on

45

days when 'Leadbitter' Jones was otherwise engaged.

On this first day of November, his morning was spent in reviewing his own affairs. He hoped he had catered sensibly for his invalid wife for whom he had provided an annuity and ownership of the house which included accommodation for the odious but essential Flora Pennington. By his own wish his son Joseph now owned the practice, with Isaac working as a salaried consultant. His Will contained bequests for Ted Baynes and Mattie, charitable gifts to the parish church, the Methodists and the hospital, and by his latest codicil, £5,000 for Kathy and £1,000 each for the two grandchildren. Some instinct (or was it a deep feeling of paternal affection?) impelled him to give Kathy a little financial independence, and he was rather pleased with the wording which accompanied his gifts to the grandchildren: 'To Rebecca, in the hope that this gift will assist her university or professional career' and 'To Daniel, for the purchase of a violin.'

At twelve thirty, his desk tidy, Isaac walked across the Close to keep a date with Ted Baynes at the club. The two men had remained great friends though they argued incessantly about politics and religion (Isaac being a Liberal in politics and a Conservative in religion and Baynes the exact reverse!). Their invariable custom was to end their meal with coffee and a game of chess. On this particular occasion, Isaac managed to checkmate his friend and buoyed up by the weather and his victory at chess, decided to call on Matilda Broadbent for tea.

It was no great distance to the hospital: he'd walked it many times in the past. But today he was walking more slowly than previously and felt unusually tired and short of breath when at last he reached the hospital.

Matty saw at once that he was very exhausted. She took him through to her private apartment, removed his overcoat and sat him down in her high-backed chair.

'Now you rest there quietly, Mr Isaac. I'll be back in a minute, but first I'll send in some tea with the thin bread and butter that you always fancy.'

'You're very kind, Matty.'

'I don't know about that,' the matron replied, 'but I admit, Isaac, you're the only governor who gets the bread-and-butter treatment.

For the others it's biscuits only. She brushed the old man's forehead with a kiss and bustled away to deal with her own business.

A staff nurse brought Isaac tea and poured a cup for him. But when Matty returned an hour later, she found her old friend breathing very heavily as if he had suffered some slight stroke. His head was propped against the wing of the chair and the teacup upset. With a sad little smile she noticed that the bread and butter had been consumed.

She raised his head, looked at his eyes, felt his pulse and rang for a nurse. Death was very close. She rang Joseph only to find he was out of the office, but Kathy was at home and rushed to the hospital.

The two women were beside Isaac Selby when he died. He didn't speak again but while Matty was phoning, the nurse had pieced together a few words uttered in gasping monosyllables: 'Danny, the music is playing for me now.'

The old man was duly interred in the Methodist burial ground close by his home beyond Holmesdale. By his own wish, his last resting place was marked by a stone lying flat to the ground, an open book at each end, and in the centre

Isaac Selby
of Melbridge
Solicitor at Law
1896–1974

Some people in Melbridge were surprised at the size of his estate, but others recalled his oft-repeated advice. 'The money you make is the money you don't spend.'

Nobody could doubt that Isaac Selby had lived a good life, true to his profession, his friends and his principles.

Kathy was surprised at the change in her husband's outlook and behaviour after his father's death. It was as if a prisoner had been set free. One morning while she was getting breakfast and Joe was dressing upstairs she heard him singing a Charles Wesley hymn remembered from childhood long ago. It began, she knew, with the question 'And can it be?' and was followed with 'my chains fell off, my heart was free.' There was no question mark about Joseph's sense of liberation.

To the wider world of Melbridge Joe's liberation was advertised by a change of business address when he moved the offices of Selby & Leadbitter into one of the Georgian houses on Southside. Joe liked to pretend that the move was a tribute to his father's sagacity – and in a sense it was, for Isaac Selby was the man who had first conceived the idea of turning the road on the southern boundary of the church land into a pedestrian precinct. Backed by Edward Baynes, and the leading people of the town, Isaac's patience and negotiating skill with planning authorities and church commissioners had brought the idea to fruition. He had even ensured that the leaseholds of this attractive row of Georgian houses should remain in suitable hands. By 1974, the Southside tenants included, in addition to the vicarage and a curate's house, Dr Latimer's surgery, the Melbridge Club, a bank, the branch of a leading Melchester estate agent, a chartered accountant and now, at long last, the legal firm of Selby & Leadbitter. It seemed entirely appropriate that Melbridge people should refer to Southside as Selby's Pavement.

Early in the New Year, Joe Selby stood at the second-floor window of his spacious new office. Over the Christmas break Owen 'Leadbitter' Jones had organised the move from Feathers Lane with great efficiency. Old Owen might be a bit long in the tooth, Joe reflected, but he was orderly by nature, as well as by training. Everything in Joe's office was in place: the big desk with the table lamp and telephone so placed that the daylight would reach Mr Joseph's swivel chair from the left and no shadow should fall on his handwriting; a new dark green carpet, with lighter green curtains to match, had been supplied and fitted by Higgins of East Street; the legal tomes on the bookshelves lining the walls were all newly dusted; and an oval mahogany table, surrounded by four matching chairs, stood in the far corner of the room.

Joe looked round his new office and liked what he saw. He must remember to give Owen and his staff a generous bonus for their extra work. And they would be better housed too – proper washing facilities and separate offices for Richard Fagg and 'Leadbitter' Jones on the first and ground floors.

He turned back to look out across the Close. What a change from the drab outlook in Feathers Lane. In the fading light the setting sun still imparted a little colour to the tiled roofs of the town. The skeletal trees and the expanse of mown grass studded by occasional grave-stones provided a fine setting for the old church standing majestic in the centre of its little kingdom.

To the north, beyond the church, he could just see the low-slung buildings of the grammar school and the new classrooms and playing fields stretching up the Melchester Road. In the west, the floodlighting on the Feathers Inn had just been switched on; and on the far side of East Street the defensive shutters were being hoisted over the shopfronts.

'There's a mint of money in East Street,' thought Joseph. 'Melbridge is too small to attract the big multiple stores. I wouldn't be surprised if that row of shops wasn't the real reason for Father's decision to set up his practice in Melbridge.'

Joe Selby may well have been right. Certain it is that since the distant days of Baedeker's recommendation to tourists, East Street had become a more cogent reason than the parish church for visiting Melbridge. You came to East Street whenever you wanted to buy something special. Gutteridge the grocer, for instance, ran a superb delicatessen department, and stocked a great variety of cheeses, cut with a wire (please taste it for yourself, madam). Hepburn, the ironmonger and tool stockist, provided a paradise for DIY experts and also specialised in model railways. The watchmaker and jeweller would value and offer a fair price for the family silver, if required. A third generation of the slightly eccentric Collingtons ran a considerable drapery business. While the stock was up to date, the family delighted in retaining such old-fashioned gadgets as the brass yardage measure lining the counter, and included the words 'milliners and haberdashers' on their letterheadings. The fishmonger, his wares sea-fresh from the Abbotshaven fishing fleet, was also a poulterer and happy to pluck the gentry's pheasants. Altogether, the East Street tradesmen of Melbridge provided a very pleasant shopping service for their customers. People from the county came to Melbridge to shop in East Street, parking their cars on ground opposite the shops and leased from the church authorities. As like as not, visitors as well as the people of Melbridge would stop in the town for morning coffee at Dolly Hayward's, or walk across the Close for lunch at the Feathers. It goes without saying that the proprietors of the East Street shops were, to a man, members of the Melbridge Club on

Southside. As the years passed, Selby & Leadbitter came to handle more and more of their legal business and became familiar with their family problems.

Joe turned away from the window; it was time to go home to his wife and children. But he hesitated as he locked his handsome front door. For a moment, he stood irresolute at the top of the steps leading down to the pavement. A passer-by, walking along Southside, might have noticed the hint of a smile on the solicitor's face – an unusual sight in a man who was careful never to betray his feelings in public.

Actually, in spite of his euphoric state of mind, Joe was puzzling over two separate and unconnected problems. First, what were they to do about Danny's future education? To Joe's way of thinking it would be disastrous for the boy to continue at the grammar school. His musical talents, unusual indeed for a boy of his age, would give him a sort of special status both in the school and in a small town like Melbridge; this must be bad for him. What he needed was a wider outlook on life, a wider circle of friends. Bob Withers, whom he had consulted, suggested moving Danny to a public school like Highminster. It might be just the place for him, Bob thought. Modelled on Arnold's Rugby, Highminster was not too far away. It was, thought Bob, more conservative than contemporary Rugby, with its advanced curricula in the fields of industry and computer technology: but still reflecting Arnold's ideal of Christian leadership. Moreover, it shared Rugby's musical reputation. Highminster sounded right for Danny.

But Joe didn't fool himself. It would be fiendishly difficult to convince Kathy, or John Lucas or that Polish *poseur*. And what of Danny himself?

Joe Selby thrust aside the question of Danny's school and turned to his second problem, which was solely concerned with the management of Selby & Leadbitter. How was he to get Richard Fagg to the office by eight forty-five a.m. each day? Joseph had always clung to his father's basic principle that the boss should never reach his business later than the official opening time. Richard, with his temporary digs in Melchester, was constantly late and would certainly affect the punctuality of the staff, unless something was done about it. The obvious answer was to persuade Richard to move to Melbridge. A fresh idea flashed into his mind. Why not persuade Mrs Grant to rent him her newly acquired premises in Feathers Lane? Without further hesitations Joe moved briskly down the steps and crossed Selby's Pavement into the Close.

He looked completely absorbed in his own thinking, as he chose the diagonal path to the West Street exit facing the Feathers. But why, why did his father's memory keep obtruding? Did the half-smile on Joseph's features contain a hint of defiance, as if to say 'I'll show him, I'll show him'? Or was he amused by the thought that he was about to enter the Feathers which his teetotal father had considered the lair of the Devil. 'Ridiculous,' thought Joe, 'absurdly dated.' Everybody except his father knew that Eleanor Grant was a model of her kind, managing a first-class establishment which provided its customers with real ale, excellent snacks and a restaurant recommended by the *Good Food Guide*.

But on reaching the Feathers something impelled him to walk past the main entrance and turn left into Feathers Lane for a last look at the dark little house where his father had first affixed his nameplate.

Once again, memory troubled him. He recalled how the old man had obstinately refused to move into more commodious premises: 'the money you make is the money you don't spend' was one of Isaac's favourite aphorisms. But surely, argued Joseph, Father would be delighted to see how well his brass plate looks in the dignity of its Southside setting? And how pleased he would be at the price Mrs Grant had paid for his dingy old office – not everybody in Melbridge knew of Mrs Grant's need for more staff accommodation. And her cash was good too. Joseph congratulated himself on his perspicacity and hoped that Mrs Grant would be a very useful new client. Yes, indeed, Joe intended to show Melbridge and its neighbourhood that he, Joseph Selby, was something more than his father's son.

They say that pride is a deadly sin from which no man is free. Certainly it invaded the mind of Mr Joseph Selby on that evening in Melbridge.

He took a final look at the old office. Then, as if in conscious defiance of his father's lifetime of abstinence, he turned on his heel and entered the bar of the Feathers from the back entrance in the lane. It was like coming from darkness into light. Joseph was almost blinded by the illuminated array of bottles and glasses displayed before his eyes. Only as he ordered a whisky from a welcoming barmaid did he become embarrassingly aware of the silence caused by his entry. Had he been more familiar with the social reactions of bar habitués he would have known that regular drinkers invariably lower their voices or break off their conversation when a stranger unexpectedly enters their familiar haunt.

His entry may have been unexpected but he was no stranger to the drinkers at an adjacent table. All four of them immediately recognised the well-built fifty-two-year-old solicitor with his steel-grey eyes and strong craggy features. In Melbridge he was even recognised by the tailored excellence of his grey suit – it was just another reflection of his father's code of conduct: 'Remember, Joseph, you'll never carry authority in this life unless you are well dressed.'

Tom Gutteridge, the East Street grocer, was the first to break the silence.

'Good evening, Mr Selby. This is a nice surprise. What brings you here?'

'Well, I want a word with Mrs Grant, and this bar –' he smiled at the drinkers – 'makes a very pleasant short cut from Feathers Lane where I've been taking a last look at our old offices before they change shape.'

Joe turned to the girl at the bar and asked her to confirm that Mrs Grant was free.

'Her Ladyship should be in her office at this time of night,' said Tom. 'Have you time for another drink first?'

Joe excused himself. 'Thank you, gentlemen, but no, not this evening, I think. Business first and then home.' With a parting gesture of regret Joe Selby left by the front exit door which opened into the hotel reception area.

'And what can we do for you, Mr Selby?' Eleanor Grant stood up to greet him. She was about the same age as the solicitor. At fifty she was still a good-looking woman with her figure nicely under control and a mind as sharp as a needle.

Joseph Selby, having negotiated the sale of the old office, knew her style. He came straight to the point.

'To be brief, Mrs Grant, I wonder if I could rent your new property in Feathers Lane.'

'Well, I'm damned,' the lady replied. 'First you sell me the property and then want it back?'

'Well not exactly, Mrs Grant. But my new assistant, Richard Fagg, really ought to be living in Melbridge.'

'And you would pay a rent commensurate with the price I paid for the property?' Eleanor Grant smiled triumphantly. The sale price asked by Joseph Selby had been pretty stiff. But a tenant suited her well, for earlier plans for housing a chef and his family had fallen through.

So Mrs Grant accepted Joe's proposal.

'I'm sure we understand each other, Mr Selby. May I leave your firm to draw up an agreement in more formal terms?'

Eleanor Grant was only too happy to oblige Mr Selby. As they parted company, they both felt sufficiently acquainted to address each other by their first names.

'Goodnight, then, Joseph.'

'Goodnight, Eleanor.'

Joseph Selby emerged from the front entrance of the Feathers to catch a bus at the junction of West Street and the Melchester Road. At least one of his problems was solved.

Back in the Feathers bar, the talk centred on Joseph Selby.

'Well, that's Joseph Selby, that was!'

'First time I've ever seen him with a glass of whisky . . . Old Isaac wouldn't have liked that.'

Higgins broke in. 'I've fitted out his new office on Southside, and I tell you, it's the tops. Whether his father would have approved is quite another matter.'

'Oh, Joe aims to step high – no doubt about it – and why not?'

'I reckon his marriage to Kathy Hardingham has made all the difference. She was in the shop the other day, buying some things for her daughter – real good-lookers, both of them.'

'And what price young Daniel? Joe will find it hard to keep up with him, I shouldn't wonder.'

There was so much to talk about in a small town. But Tom Gutteridge looked at his watch. It was time to go home.

They waved farewell to the barmaid.

'Goodnight, Betsie luv – see you tomorrow.'

'Goodnight, gentlemen. Goodnight.'

From Edward Baynes' Diary, 1975

I miss old Isaac more than I can express in words. Silly really . . . What more can a man wish for a friend than that he should die in the fullness of years, without pain, in a place he loves and with a firm faith in eternal life? Yet Isaac's death leaves a gap in my life which cannot be bridged. The chessmen stand idle on the antique chequerboard table which he gave to the Melbridge Club, and I am deprived of the stimulus of his political and theological observations. This small town, too, has lost a man who was, in the words of St Francis, 'an instrument of God's peace'. Indeed, the council has immediately recognised his contribution to the harmony of its life by changing the name of the Southside pedestrian precinct into Selby's Pavement.

His dedication to peace extended into his home as well as his public life. I never heard him complain about Rachel and Flora Pennington, though they brought him little comfort at the end of the day.

Yet I sometimes wonder how far Rachel's withdrawal from Melbridge life affected the only son's relationship with his parents. When I prepared Joseph for confirmation, I suspected that his over-riding desire was to escape into a world less constricted than his Plymouth Brethren home. Indeed, his marriage to Kathy Hardingham seemed to be part of the same process.

Perhaps old Isaac understood his son's motives. Certainly, he loved Joe's young bride as his own daughter – a substitute for the affection he could no longer feel for his invalid wife.

But I think he also hoped that Kathy and her young family would act as a brake on his son's ambition. As I write this the town is talking about Joe's expensive new office and his commissions from Lord Melchester which have forced him to hire a salaried man with no knowledge of Melbridge ways to take much of the local work off his shoulders. But he's still working so hard that he has no spare time to give to his wife and children. I give no credence to the gossip about Kathy and young Carstairs. But instinct and a priest's experience of family troubles warn me that there could be rough water ahead for the Selby family.

8

As Joe left the bus and turned from the Melchester Road towards 10 Ockenham Drive, he was irritated – and not for the first time – by the similarity of the twenty 'desirable residences' in this 'no thorough-fare' road. What he and Kathy had thought 'desirable' seventeen years ago satisfied him no longer. There was nothing to distinguish the Selby home at number ten from the nineteen other houses in the Drive, apart from the neatness of the front garden which was one of Kathy's special delights.

The sight set off a nagging train of thought which would not go away. Was Ockenham Drive the right address for Mr and Mrs Joseph Selby? With the growing demand for these 'four bed, all mod, con., small garden' houses, should they not put number ten on the market and make a killing? The idea suited his mood. Change, upward change, was drawing him inexorably forward. But what would Kathy think? Perhaps he could find a house of individual character which would really take her fancy? Something with easy access to the town? Something close to the river, in the same area as the Latimers' newly acquired place? Maybe he should have a word with Bob Withers. From time to time, houses of considerable character came up for sale on the Melchester estate, didn't they? And supposing His Lordship wanted to retain ownership, renting a house from a good landlord could have its attractions. Like retaining the use of the capital gained from selling number ten? He checked himself as he reached his front door. It was no good going too far on his own. Everything depended on his lovely Kathy. 'Choose your moment carefully,' he told himself. 'There's a time to speak, and a time for silence.'

Kathy's welcoming quick kiss, and enquiry whether he had had a good day, and his 'What's for supper?' were followed by a rush down the stairs as Danny broke away from his homework to greet his father. He was joined by Rebecca who was enjoying her half term break from Melchester High.

But tonight was different as Kathy smelt the whisky on Joe's breath. 'Had a drinking evening, Joe? What would your father say?' Kathy was allowed to laugh at Joe, and often did so if he looked like getting pompous.

She was, however, genuinely surprised at his explanation.

'OK, Joe, I am sure that opening a new office demands a little celebration, but why at the Feathers? And why alone? And what about the rest of the staff and the family?'

'Well, my love, I wanted a word with Eleanor Grant.'

'Eleanor, eh? So we're on Christian name terms with "Her Ladyship", are we?'

'Cross my heart, Kathy, that's the truth. I think I've persuaded Her Ladyship, as you call her, to rent our old office to Richard Fagg. It's not good for the office staff to see him turning up late each day – always making excuses about the Melchester traffic. But no more business tonight. Tomorrow will be time enough for you to inspect the new office on Southside.'

After supper, Danny went to play his hi-fi music equipment and Becky retired to the kitchen where she was trying out some cake recipe given her by a schoolfriend.

Left alone, Joe and Kathy immediately reverted to the thorny subject of Danny's education.

'I'm sure, Kathy, that Danny needs a change of scene.'

'But why, Joe? He's doing well under John Lucas. He's getting marvellous violin tuition from Professor Podolski. He's going through a very sensitive stage and he'll hate boarding school. You've got Highminster in mind, haven't you?'

'You mustn't worry about that side of things. Today, public schools are fully accustomed to coping with new boys who have never been away from home. I'm told they fit in ever so quickly.'

'How do you know?' There was an aggressive note in Kathy's voice.

'Well, Bob Withers . . .'

Joe got no further. Kathy was at him again. 'It's always Bob

Withers these days. I know. He was at Blundell's and the agricultural place at Cirencester. Actually I like him. He's a nice chap, but about as different from Danny as chalk from cheese. You'll be telling me next that he knows the Highminster headmaster.'

Joe remained outwardly unruffled, almost offensively judicial.

'Well, my dear, I would have made that point, or something like it, had you let me finish my sentence. The fact is that a Blundell's friend of Bob, Roger Powell by name, is a housemaster at Highminster and he's told Bob to tell us there's a music scholarship Danny could sit for next month.'

'And what do our Melbridge friends say? John Lucas for instance, and the vicar?' Kathy was rapidly losing her temper. 'I don't believe you're thinking of Danny's future at all. You're obsessed with this old-school-tie racket and the sort of social tag that you think it still commands. According to my father, that sort of class snobbery is disappearing so fast you can't see it for dust. I know solicitors have to deal with all sorts of clients. But would you honestly hold up Lord Melchester as an object for imitation?'

Joe was about to reply that Lord Melchester had no connection with Highminster or Danny when Rebecca burst into the room.

'What on earth's come over you two? I can hear nearly every word in the kitchen and I've never known you so bad tempered. Look, everybody knows – and that includes Danny – that you're arguing about changing his school. Well, why not declare a truce, let him enter for this music scholarship and see what happens?

'No, not another word.' Becky stopped both her parents from starting the argument again. 'I can't stand rows.'

She turned back to the kitchen. 'Give me thirty seconds and I'll let you sample the chocolate cake I've just made.'

The outcome was predictable. Joseph, with Becky's help, won the day. In spite of Kathy's reservations and the disapproval of John Lucas, Danny sat for the music scholarship at Highminster, liked the look of the school buildings ('spacious, Mum, not like myopic Melbridge') and was delighted when he won the scholarship, way ahead of the other competitors.

In September his parents drove him over to the new school, and felt greatly reassured by the interview they had with Danny's housemaster who was indeed Bob Withers' old schoolfriend. Kathy, in particular, was charmed by Roger Powell. After a quick introduction, the latter summoned another boy and sent him off to show Danny round the House.

'It's easier that way,' Mr Powell said. 'All boys hate twiddling their thumbs while their parents are in conversation with a schoolmaster.' Then he answered their queries.

Yes, there were many boys entering the school who had no previous experience of boarding school, but they fell into the school routine remarkably quickly. Taken by and large, they lived such a full life that they found no time to be homesick. That, he hoped, would be true of Daniel who would be receiving special violin and piano tuition, additional to his normal school work.

In answer to a question from Joe, Mr Powell also confirmed that Daniel had sent in some excellent Common Entrance papers, including an outstanding English essay.

'One always wonders, Mr Selby, whether we've placed a boy too high or too low on the strength of his entrance exams; but I hope we've guessed correctly in Daniel's case. Actually, that lad who is taking your son round the house is in the same form and will be sharing a study with him. Name of Peter Wrattenley,' he added, and turned to Kathy. 'Known to one and all as Ratty: a shortening of his family name, Mrs Selby, and no reference to *The Wind in the Willows*, though I sometimes think he shares some of the virtues of Grahame's water rat. In other words, I shall be surprised and sad if the two of them don't hit it off pretty well.'

Very soon, the boys were back from their tour and together they accompanied Joe and Kathy to the car. A quick, unsentimental farewell – 'Goodbye, Dad, goodbye, Mum – see you soon' – and Kathy, looking through her driving mirror, saw Ratty and Daniel hurrying away into their new school world.

Danny's first year at Highminster could be more or less accurately charted by the weekly letter that junior boys were expected to write each Saturday.

For most of them, the objective was to fill the page as quickly as possible, and get it addressed and posted. One well-known dodge was to list members of the First XV with initials and relevant Houses added – a frightful bore for Mother but, of course, 'it showed keenness' according to one of the dodgers whose father had once been at the school.

Danny, who enjoyed writing and was quite uninhibited, took a different view. The first letters home, addressed to Mum and Dad, were exactly what you would expect:

> Yes, I'm getting on fine, thank you. Peter Wrattenley, the boy who showed me round the House, shares a study with me. Everybody calls him Ratty. We get on fine. He's related to a peer, but that doesn't seem to matter. He came to my rescue the other day when a boy threw a wet sponge at me while I was saying my prayers – you're supposed to say your prayers between cleaning your teeth and lights-out. Ratty was after my attacker like a tiger. He pinioned his shoulders to the ground and began to knock the fellow's head on the floorboards to a pleasant rhythmic beat: 'Don't you ever do such a thing again.' See what I mean? 'Dum, dum/diddy dum/ diddy dum/de dum.' The commotion came to a sudden halt when Winthrop came in. He's a 'big shot' and the prefect in charge of our dorm. Everybody hopped into bed double quick, I can tell you. I'll tell you more about Winthrop in my next letter.

And so he did. From the explosive, telling phrases which boys so often employ as if they were out of breath or running late, Joe and Kathy received a clear pen-picture of the great man: 'Tall, fair hair, in the school sides for rugger, hockey and cricket. I'm his fag and his Christian name is Guy.'

There was also a postscript. 'I've taken Ratty's advice and say my prayers under the bedclothes. As Ratty says, "God can hear you loud and clear whether you are in bed or out of it."'

In the sixth week of term, Danny 'broke radio silence' to use his own words. A letter reached number ten, stamped UNCENSORED in red ink, the word composed on one of those old-fashioned printing sets with India rubber letters.

> I've an overwhelming urge to put you right about the horrible game of Rugby football which Highminster makes everybody play unless he has a medical certificate like Ratty. I have now

played a sufficient number of times to assure you that this game
has been invented by savages for savages. I do not exaggerate.
There's a world famous side called the Barbarians and that
word (remember, Dad?) was coined by the Romans to describe
and comprehend all the uncivilised tribes who lived outside and
beyond the boundaries of the civilised world. Self-confessed
savages, you see?

But back to your son's grizzly fate among the savages!
Because I'm a bit below average height but have strong
forearms, I've been ordered to play at scrum-half. As I cannot
wear spectacles, I don't see much of the game. But if the ball
comes out of the scrum through eight pairs of legs, I'm
expected to get hold of the ball and throw a long pass to our fly-
half. In next to no time, somebody drops the ball, the referee
orders another scrum and this tedious progression continues
until the final whistle.

If the opposition succeeds in 'heeling' the ball I remain in
comparative safety. But if our men get the ball I am attacked by
two enormous louts who rush round the scrum and kick me
unmercifully in order to get the ball out of my hands. It really *is*
a horrible game. I long for next term and hockey which I used
to enjoy at Melbridge and where I can at least wear my
spectacles and see what's going on.

In the meantime please pray for my survival (joke) and tear
up this letter (serious). According to Highminster's unwritten
laws, criticism of Rugby football is little short of high treason!

The treasonable document proved prophetic. In the following week
the housemaster, Roger Powell, rang Melbridge to say that Danny
had damaged his left hand.

'No broken bones I'm glad to say, Mr Selby, but no more rugger,
I'm afraid, for Daniel this term. Rotten luck. But the school medical
officer and my house matron both report that Daniel is taking this
setback with a humorous resignation which has greatly impressed
them. Good for Daniel.

'It means, of course, that he will not play a piano or violin until
the hand mends, but we are arranging for a physiotherapist to help
him. As for exercise, he'll be allowed to go on walks with his

friend Peter Wrattenley, who is off games at the moment.

'I'm so sorry to bring you this news but I would like you to know that Daniel has made a very good start at Highminster and will certainly be moved to a higher form next term.'

Danny's next Sunday letter gave a slightly different version of the accident.

> Great news. Rejoice, I say again, rejoice. A lout has trodden so hard on my left hand that I can't play rugger again this term. The school doctor seems a good chap, his physiotherapist is reckoned rather tough as women go, and Matron is a dear old sweetie, a bit like Mattie, who brings me hot drinks when I visit her. I've had another visitor – Mrs Powell, my housemaster's wife. About your age, Mum, and nearly as good to look on. I'm also told that she's a jolly good pianist. We may get together when I am ready to play the fiddle again. No more now. Only five weeks before I am back at Melbridge. Meanwhile, shout for joy that your son and heir is enjoying his convalescence. Tell Harry Leng to play Psalm 150.

9

Two scenes from the Christmas holidays stuck in Danny's mind as he returned to Highminster for the spring term. The first was Christmas Day itself: the opening of the family presents, with a super evening dress for Becky and for himself the recording of Beethoven's nine symphonies conducted by Klemperer; then the walk to the parish church across the Close on a brisk frosty morning with the trees leafless and the dew on the grass sparkling in the sunshine; the warmth and the welcome of the great church which he knew so well; and on by car to Holmesdale village and Buckley's where Grandma Hardingham had provided a splendid feast. No place, thought Danny, could provide a more lovely setting for Christmas than his own home town.

And then, in the New Year, came the London expedition to buy the violin which Grandpa Selby's legacy had made possible. It was a great day also for Jan Podolski and for Kathy and Rebecca who were included in the party. After an hour of testing and bargaining in an obscure little shop off the Charing Cross Road, the Professor announced that he and Danny had acquired the finest violin this side of Cremona.

'And now,' the Professor announced, 'we celebrate in true Polish style.' He whizzed them off in a taxi to a famous Polish restaurant in the West End and led his party to a reserved table with that same air of authority he had shown at last year's concert. He looked as if he owned the place, as he rapped out an order to the waiter to tell the chef des cuisines that Podolski had arrived. Then, to the astonishment of the other diners, the two men had embraced with a flurry of Polish greetings which clearly indicated that a nostalgic reunion between very old friends was taking place.

The Professor, with Polish vodka in his hand, ordered the meal.

'A fruit cocktail for mademoiselle, yes? And for my good colleague, yes? And for madame, dry sherry, yes? And now food. All like beetroot, ye-es? Four Bortsch. Next, Dover sole – the reason, dear lady, why so many emigrés choose England for home. So, Jurek,' he turned to the chef, 'four Sole Meunière and no bones, mind. I do not take bones with fish. And for finish? Perhaps a Marie Walewska! But maybe we pause for further thought.'

'But Professor,' Kathy protested, 'I don't think . . .'

The Professor held up his hand imperiously. 'Madame Kathy, I *give* this meal in token of friendship: it is my pleasure. But, between ourselves, it costs me nothing! It is repayment for Polish debt of honour.'

During the soup course, he explained how the debt of honour had been incurred. The chef, once a barrister of the High Court of Warsaw, had joined the violinist from Cracow University at Pastrudi's famous restaurant in Alexandria, to celebrate their great escape across Eastern Europe to enrol in General Anders' 2nd Polish Corps. On this memorable occasion the Professor from Cracow had paid the bill.

'Strange how the world goes upside down,' concluded the Professor. 'In 1942 barrister's pocket is empty but musician is earning much money from cafés and generous British boys, you see. Today situation is reversed. Barrister turns cook and is very rich: musician stays with violin, his first love, and lives poor. Barrister-chef most happy to repay his debt.'

Back at Highminster, Danny was telling Peter Wrattenley about his Polish celebratory lunch, spiced with all the exaggerations common to schoolboy stories. A crowd collected and began to laugh as a mêlée of nonsense burst from the Wrattenley/Selby study. 'I, Podolski, command it . . . all like beetroot, ye-es . . . Polish soup *wunderbar* . . . Next, Dover sole, but remember *mon vieux* . . . Podolski no eat bones with fish, *eh*? No, naiver . . . and to finish . . . (there was a luscious kissing sound) ze Marie Walewska ice cream. Fantastic!'

The crowd in the passage were shouting, 'Do it again, Selby! I, Podolski, command it,' when the nine o'clock bell for prayers effectively ended the performance. There was, however, a sequel at the midday meal on the following Friday (invariably fish day in Powell's House) when a boy holding up a bone extracted from the fish pie shouted to Danny, 'This is bad show, Selby. I, Podolski, naiver eat bones with fish – no, naiver.'

It was at this time that Ratty began to notice the two sides to his study mate's character – sometimes moody and reserved, sometimes extrovert and exhibitionist. A few weeks after the Podolski incident, a young history master told the form that a political debate would take place on the following Tuesday and called for volunteers to present the case for the main political parties. Conservative? The son of the Conservative member for West Wiltshire raised his hand. Labour? A Birmingham boy, son of a regional TUC boss, immediately volunteered. Liberal? Dead silence until some wit proposed Podolski Selby – 'He always thinks differently from the rest of us, sir.' The master turned to the smallish boy with the spectacles sitting silent at the back of the class. 'Well, what about it, Selby?'

'Anything you say, sir, provided the electorate understands that I am totally English on both sides of my family.'

The master smiled. 'Thank you, Selby, and here's your reward. You and your fellow speakers are excused the essay which the rest of the form will be writing on "Parliament and the Start of the English Civil War".'

Tuesday came. The Conservative and Labour representatives presented their cases. It was Danny's turn.

He started by congratulating the two previous speakers on the fluency with which they had reflected the views of their respective parents. 'I suggest,' he concluded, 'we leave them to uphold the "never change anything" tradition of this great school, while the rest of us actually *think* for *ourselves*.'

The shaft struck home. The class came to life. They were listening hard as Danny briefly listed the twentieth-century reforms which stemmed from Liberal thinking: pensions and Lloyd George; the Keynes revolution in the Government's use of money; Beveridge and National Health Insurance. Churchill arguing entry into Europe (an angry murmur of, 'He wasn't a Liberal,' silenced by a crisp reply to the speaker to study the composition of the Liberal Cabinet of 1906); and Churchill's European policy endorsed by Liberals in the early fifties, 'while the two main parties were fast asleep.'

'All this, and shares for those who work in the factories! So why, I ask, does this country not vote Liberal to a man and a woman? First, because the Liberals are poor. They rely on their own members for money. They have no big brother, the City or trade unions or newspaper proprietors to prop them up. Secondly, because the voting system is still "first past the post" and not proportional representation as used by other countries who prefer true democracy to class leadership.'

He made one final point. 'Some will say that PR may mean coalition government. But why are they so fearful? Have they forgotten that in 1914 and 1939 our victories were gained under coalition governments led by David Lloyd George and Winston Churchill? So please, I beg you, *think* for yourselves and stop accepting as gospel truth the loaded falsehoods churned out *ad nauseam* by the City, the Tory-owned papers and the Trade Union Congress.'

Danny sat down – a Danny unknown to his schoolfriends, but easily recognised by those who had once heard him sing the Schubert lied at Melbridge. Somehow or other, without raising his voice but using his spectacles so that he seemed to be addressing himself to each member of the form personally, Danny ended by winning a clear majority of the votes.

Honours followed: a Headmaster's Distinction and a special note from Roger Powell who also wrote to Joseph Selby about his son's success. The parents were baffled when another 'uncensored' letter arrived by the same post as the housemaster's letter.

Dear Mum and Dad,
I had a bit of luck the other day. Some idiot in the new form, trying to be funny, proposed me as a Liberal spokesman in a political debate staged by our history master (whom I rather like). So I took on the job though I shall not decide how to vote until I'm eighteen! Anyhow, I treated the form to all that guff the English master at Melbridge used to spout – remember, Dad, he used to sing in the choir and describe himself as 'the last Liberal in Melbridge'. But here's the point, I also suggested that the class should break loose from Highminster's 'no

change' traditions and think for themselves. And – believe it or not – I won the day.

But seriously, I don't know how long I can stand all this tradition business. Silly rules – no hands in pockets however cold you are; no umbrellas unless you're in the Lower Sixth, however hard it rains – everybody dressed alike; everybody trained to govern an Empire which disappeared in 1945! See what I mean? This school is a hundred years out of date.

I'm not short of friends – and Ratty is great. So why am I so fed up? I think it's something in the blood – born and bred a non-conformist (social, not religious!) and descended in a straight line from Grandpa Selby's Plymouth Brethren.

Perhaps, we can talk more about it when I'm back at Melbridge.

Joe and Kathy looked at each other.

'What do we do, Joe? It looks as if Highminster's not going to work.'

'Do, Kathy? I think we wait till the holidays. Once we've talked with the boy, we might have a word with Roger Powell. I do, at least, know what Danny means about that "non-conformist" streak. It's in my blood, too.'

In fact, Roger Powell pre-empted Joe Selby's idea by driving over to Melbridge with his wife, Diana.

They had made a social visit to Bob Withers an excuse for dropping in on the Selbys in Ockenham Drive – partly to discuss Danny's start at Highminster, but chiefly because Diana Powell wanted Danny's help with a soirée she was going to hold in the summer term.

'I wondered whether Daniel and one of his friends would join us and then play something for us. I would be happy to act as his accompanist.'

Roger Powell was amused and surprised by Danny's ready acceptance of the invitation (in Roger's book, boys of fifteen were extremely wary of such commitments). But Diana was delighted. That very same day, Danny collected the score of a Mozart sonata for violin and piano from Jan Podolski in Abbotshaven and Roger promised to arrange special practice times with the school's director of music.

The latter had hitherto failed to win the music scholar's approval. 'No soul, Mum; a sort of piano automaton. We call him Count Czerny after that ghastly chap who wrote all those exercises you had to practise at Melchester High.'

But once back for the summer term at Highminster, Danny was a little less critical. 'Count Czerny,' he wrote, 'is being quite helpful to Diana P. and me. The fact is he desperately wants to claim a bit of credit for the show, especially as the Powells' guests will include the headmaster and his wife in addition to one or two notables from the town. So cross your fingers, everybody. I think Diana will be OK – funny really that I have to give her confidence, whereas, last year, it was Jan Podolski helping me.'

In the event, the Mozart went well, and, for good measure, they played Sarasate's *Zapapeado*, one of Heifetz's favourite encores. Ratty turned the pages for Diana Powell and reported to his friends in the House that the housemaster's wife looked fabulous.

And 'Podolski-Selby'?

'Out of this world, old boy, out of this world . . . the audience stopped talking and drinking . . . at the end, Selby bowed to Diana and kissed her hand! What a chap!'

Daniel's version was somewhat different. 'Before the show, the food was terrific and then Ratty kept Diana on course . . . she never made a mistake . . . and afterwards Ratty and I managed to get a glass of Sauterne which the guests had enjoyed with the sweets.'

'Did the headmaster or Roger see you?' Daniel went into top gear. 'How should I know? I, Podolski, commanded Sauterne for lovely Diana. My friend and I cannot let lady drink alone . . . would not be in Polish tradition . . . Sauterne with strawberries . . . *Wunderbar!*'

Ratty had invited Danny to stay at his home in the Lake District for the first fortnight of the summer holidays. All Danny need do was to catch the Royal Scot to Preston where Ratty and his father would meet the train. The two friends discussed their plans on a Sunday walk as they made their way to the transport café which Ratty had discovered earlier in the year.

It had remained on a curve of the old road after the new dual carriageway from Bristol had been constructed. Hidden by trees but designated as a parking place, it was well known to the old hands on the road. As for Mrs Brown (or Mother B. as the boys called her) she was always glad to see them. 'If only,' said Ratty, 'she could teach the House butler how to make tea in an urn like she makes it.'

No more 'uncensored' letters reached 10 Ockenham Drive, although there was an excited letter saying that the South of England Symphony Orchestra would be visiting Highminster in the Christmas term and Count Czerny and Danny's violin teacher hoped Danny would be allowed to play the solo part in Tchaikovsky's violin concerto. ('Remember that disc, Mum, with Isaac Stern and the Philadelphia Orchestra – the violin dominating the orchestra from the very first bar?')

It almost seemed as if this traditional public school would be able to accommodate its eccentric non-conformist pupil. Danny had rather enjoyed 'fagging' for Winthrop, and it amused him to do little unasked extras, like putting new blotting paper in Winthrop's blotting pad and persuading Matron to sew a new bit of black elastic on the great man's umbrella ('We can't have our gentleman leaving the House badly dressed, can we, Matron?'). Four days from the end of term, Danny poked his head into Guy Winthrop's study to report that he'd duly delivered a note from Winthrop to the school cricket captain.

He was standing at the door when Winthrop said, 'You give me and the House a lot of amusement, young Selby. Why don't I know more about you? Sit down and tell me more.' Winthrop pulled him against his chair. 'That's better, isn't it?'

'What do you want to know?'

'Oh, your Christian name (I know it's not Podolski), where you live. Any brothers or sisters? Any ideas about your future? Just so that I know a bit more about this anonymous musician who has looked after me so well.'

Winthrop was lying back in his old wicker chair with its flattened cushions that Danny used to rearrange each week. His left hand lightly riffled the natural wave of the boy's hair. He changed position slightly and his right hand began to steal across the boy's thigh.

Danny's reaction was swift as lightning. He wriggled free, reached the door, mumbled something about finishing an essay for tomorrow's first lesson, and streaked away up the passage to the study he shared with Peter Wrattenley. White faced and out of breath, he flung himself into a chair.

Ratty was shaken by his friend's appearance.

'My God, Danny, what's hit you? Calm down and tell me what's happened.'

But Danny was not to be drawn. Insistently, a well-remembered Latin tag was hammering in his mind. 'If you want to keep quiet about something tell nobody.'

'It's OK, Ratty. Nothing's the matter. Nothing at all. I'm fine now, honest I am. Let's get back to the holiday plans we were discussing last night. I think I must go home before joining you in the Lakes, if only to get rid of these school clothes. But I'll phone you my day and time of arrival as soon as I can. Actually, Mum can't pick me up by car, so I'm planning to go home by bus. Something different from the Volvos, Audis and Mercedes, eh? After all, it really is idiotic to return to Melbridge via Waterloo.'

Back in bed that night, Danny lay awake for a long time.

'Winthrop.' He kept repeating the name to himself. 'Guy Winthrop...' So there was some truth, was there, in that whispered talk about Winthrop. Well, he'd have none of it. He would not say a word to anybody ... not to Ratty, not to Mum and Dad, not to anybody... He would sort this thing out in his own way. By himself? Yes, that was the answer. By himself ... away from friends and parents ... away from Winthrop – away from Highminster. Get clear away. And why not by bus? The idea appealed to him. The open road. Over the hills and far away? And then an even better idea struck him. He may have smiled as his imagination soared until, at last, his eyes closed.

10

At six thirty a.m. on the day when Highminster School was breaking up for the summer holidays, Joe Selby was serving early morning tea to a somnolent Kathy at 10 Ockenham Drive. This daily tea-making was the only domestic chore that Joe performed but his timing never varied. The cup of tea reached his wife simultaneously with the BBC news summary, prayer for the day and weather forecast. From seven fifteen until eight fifteen a.m. Joe washed, shaved, dressed and breakfasted, before a brisk walk across the Church Close would bring him to his new office at eight twenty-five precisely. Joe observed this timetable with the devotion of a drill sergeant – and his family followed suit. 'Saves time and worry, you see, Kathy.'

It will be noted that there was an interval of some fifteen minutes after the BBC weather forecast, during which Joseph and Kathy would discuss the day ahead. On this particular morning Kathy, who was vaguely wondering when Danny would reach Melbridge on his cross-country bus journey, was startled to hear Joe telling her that he was thinking of taking up golf.

'Golf, Joe? Who on earth has put that idea into your head?'

'Well, I reckon I need more exercise . . . got to keep fit, you know . . . I thought, perhaps, you might like to join me . . . what do you say?'

'But Joe, a round of golf takes up a lot of time . . . the course at Abbotshaven is five miles away and overcrowded with visitors. The only alternative is that little nine-hole course nearly fifteen miles away in North Melchester.'

Kathy looked at her husband. She was wide awake now. She knew he was hiding something from her. Perhaps all lawyers were equally devious.

'Out with it, Joe. Golf could be a good idea. But somebody has put the idea into your head. You know perfectly well it has nothing to do with your health or your weight. Just put me in the picture.'

Joseph laughed. 'OK, my darling, but remember, this item is top secret. The fact is that Bob Withers and I are having an interview today with a golf course architect to decide whether the Melchester land between the bypass and the city might not make a first-class eighteen-hole course.'

'Don't tell me, Joe, that His Lordship's short of cash.'

'I'm not saying another word, love, until Bob and I are clear about the size and cost of the project. But there's no doubt in my mind that Melbridge, and Melchester for that matter, needs an easily accessible eighteen-hole golf course: and if it goes forward as Bob Withers hopes, the expanding firm of Selby & Leadbitter will have a lot of work to do. But remember, for the moment, this is still under wraps.'

While his father and mother were talking golf, Danny was making a precipitate descent to Ratty's friend at the transport café. The boy had made his plans with considerable care. The cross-country bus journey from Highminster to Melbridge was a 'blind' – 'much more fun and much cheaper', he had glibly told his parents and friends, than travelling by train to Paddington and crossing to Waterloo for the Melchester train. But he had no intention of going home. Some instinct told him that it would be best to make use of Ratty's invitation to stay in the Lake District until the school problem had been sorted out. Of one thing he was certain. Nothing – nobody – would induce him to return to Highminster.

His plan was already under way. His trunk had been forwarded to Melbridge by road-carrier, leaving him free to travel light with a rucksacks and his violin. He'd left the local bus at a request stop just before the B road from Highminster bridged the road between Melksham and Bath. He was poised for descent to Mrs Brown's transport café which was sited at the foot of a steep wooded slope, on a disused section of the former main road. It was an establishment much favoured by the older truckers who knew, from long experience, the quality of Mrs Brown's provision. The latter was just opening up when Danny landed at her feet, triumphantly holding his violin case above his head. Somehow, having lost the path through the woods that Ratty had shown him, he'd landed noisily at the caravan stall, sliding the last ten yards on his bottom.

Mrs Brown looked him up and down.

'And what in God's name are you doing here at this time o' the morning, young man? No need to introduce yourself; I've a good memory. You're Ratty's friend from the big school, aren't you?' She eyed him again. 'Just look at your trousers: you'll fair catch it from your ma, if you turn up like that. 'Alf a mo – I'll find you a brush. We only serve respectable customers in this woodland glade!'

After brushing himself down under her direction, Danny posed for her approval and made a slight bow.

'Well Mrs B., my first need is for a cup of your very special tea.'

'Now, don't you try flattery on me, young man. Making urn tea taste good is an art my old man learnt as an army cook. And, whatever your mate Ratty thinks, your man at the school will never learn 'ow to do it. Urn's on, cuppa'll be ready in a mo'. So what's next?'

'Next, I have to get a lift to Preston and I wonder if you can help. I don't want to waste time hopping lifts to junction 16 in order to find someone heading north.'

Mrs Brown eyed him again, her arms akimbo. 'And why Preston? Don't tell me you live up there.'

'You're right, of course, Mrs B. But Ratty has invited me to stay with him and his father in the Lake District – and Preston station is where they'll pick me up by car.'

'Well,' Mrs Brown's face betrayed her feelings as clearly as a weathercock indicates the way of the wind, 'it so happens as you're in luck, son. My old mate from Preston will be coming along very soon for his "eggs and B" and dripping toast. 'E's spent the night in the big ten-ton diesel down there which 'e calls Alexander.'

'And what's his name, Mrs B?'

'Officially it's Mr 'Erbert 'Arbottle. They say 'is wife calls 'im Bert. But up and down the road, the truckers refer to 'im as the Sergeant Major. If they know him well they may call 'im Sarge. Put it another way: I calls 'im Sarge, but you stick to Sergeant Major. S'that clear?

'It's up to you to make your number. The Sergeant Major rather likes someone to talk to on long journeys, but 'e's fussy as to who 'e takes on board. Chaps with long greasy 'air or sandals or dirty 'ands 'aven't an 'ope. 'E's coming along now – give them pants another brush while I look after 'Is Lordship's bacon and eggs.'

Mr Herbert Harbottle was striding towards the caravan from the ten-tonner parked at the end of the lay-by. Danny watched him as he drew near – a big man about the same age as Father he guessed: broad shouldered, clean shaven, hair going grey, light of foot, humorous eyes. Danny's mind suddenly recalled the Gospel description of the Roman centurion – 'a man having authority'.

The Sergeant Major appeared in high good humour. 'Top of the morning Mother B. Breakfast ready?' He turned to Danny. 'And you, laddie. You here for breakfast too?'

Danny was about to reply when the old lady shouted down from her cooking. 'You won't believe it, Sarge, but he wants to get to Preston. Seems OK to me, nice and polite – and plays the violin.'

'Violin, eh?' Bert Harbottle turned to Danny. 'Give us a tune, then, sonny.'

Danny had his violin out of the case – he'd do a lot for a straight run to Preston – and off he went with a spirited rendering of 'Greensleeves'.

'That were first rate. Another breakfast for the lad, Mother B; and sandwiches for both of us. We'll need a break before Preston.'

And so it came about that, fortified by an excellent breakfast, the bespectacled curly-headed youngster hopped up beside the Sergeant Major and headed for the North.

'Never been north of the Watford Gap, eh?' Mr Harbottle believed in straight questions.

'Actually, Sergeant Major, I've never travelled north of London, and that visit was to buy a violin . . . No, not the one you heard, but a special one I keep at home.'

'So you're not aiming for home today? Well, I'd better give you my schedule for the day – and see how it fits in with yours. But first, what's your name? Daniel Selby? Right, I'll call you Danny. And you call me "CSM" which is short for Company Sergeant Major. OK?'

At that point, the Sergeant Major 'briefed' his travelling companion. They'd be driving more or less due north, so no trouble with the sun. The journey would take three and a half hours, with a break at the Keele service station on the M6 to eat Mother Brown's sandwiches, stretch the legs and have a pee. Once they reached Preston, he could drop Danny on the outskirts of the town, or, if Danny preferred, he could travel as far as the factory area where Alexander would be off-loaded.

'In that case – I can take you on to the town centre in my own car. It might be the quickest way.'

'Sounds marvellous,' said Danny. 'Thanks awfully. I'd be most grateful if you could get me to the town centre.' For the first time in his runaway adventure, he began to consider his next step. Clearly he must telephone Ratty's father. But where from? And the delay in the journey might mean finding a bed in Preston. He'd get an idea soon. Meanwhile he'd keep the CSM talking. 'Tell me, who is Alexander?'

'Well, now, you'll have to listen to one of my army stories. I was drafted overseas, you see, to join a mob of Londoners who knew how to fire their 3.7-inch guns but had never been taught to drive the big Scammels which would pull their blessed guns from site to site. So they call on a depot of Lancashire bus drivers, including Herbert Harbottle. We mix with these Londoners easy enough and they include a schoolmaster chap who gives us talks on ancient history – well, it's dead boring in the desert. And there was this story about Alexander the Great marching all over the Middle East just like what we was doing. So I named my Scammel after him, see? The other lads did the same – Pharaoh, Julius Caesar, Mark Antony and so on. So now, whenever I'm driving one of the big trucks, I call 'em Alexander – or Alex, for short. Makes 'em seem a bit more human, if you see what I mean.'

Alexander the Great! Danny was ecstatic.

'It's a brilliant name for a big truck. Sitting up here with you, I feel a bit like Alexander myself – yes, Alexander riding into India on an elephant!'

'Make up any story you like, Danny, but I've got to keep my eyes on the road. Still, I may as well tell you something about the passing scene, as you've never been in these parts before.'

In the next hour, Danny was totally absorbed, as the CSM passed on snatches of information. They were not using the unfinished M5 but would be skirting Gloucester, then on through West Bromwich, but avoiding Birmingham and only joining M6 at junction 8. Just to the west of this route was the loveliest unspoilt scenery in the whole of England – yes, the CSM had seen it while he was stationed at Oswestry . . . There was a sudden halt in the recital, an angry burst on Alexander's horn, and the application of his hydraulic brakes. 'You silly bastard,' the CSM was shouting in the direction of a sports car which had entered the motorway from the left and crossed in front of Alexander to reach the outer fast lane. The CSM was silent for a moment. Then he turned to Danny. 'You saw what that fool did? How did he know what was coming up on the outside lane? You watch it, Danny, when you're old enough to drive. Never do a thing like that if you want a long life.'

A few minutes later, they turned into the Keele service station.

'Twenty minutes' stop, Danny. First, the Gents; then I get my own teapot filled with boiling water and you unpack Mother B's sandwiches. Right? And here's sugar and fresh milk.' Herbert Harbottle was an orderly man and a man of taste who preferred his Assam tea to anonymous teabags.

'Alexander the Great' would have cleared the service area on schedule, but for an appeal for help from another trucker. Could the CSM help a bloke who couldn't get his diesel started and had to keep a date on Merseyside?

A full hour passed before Mr Harbottle climbed back into his driver's seat.

'Sorry about the delay, but I don't like backing away and saying I've no time. You never know when you may have a bit of trouble yourself. We'll still make Preston by teatime.'

And so they did, travelling at a steady 65 mph until they reached the outskirts of the town. They crossed the Ribble ('a sizeable stream, Danny, that you've probably never heard of') and then made for the BAC factory in Strand Road where the CSM signed off. He told Danny he would be engaged next day on another overnight trip, so he was leaving most of his personal gear on board. But he removed what he called his 'ditty bag' and with Danny sitting beside him and nursing his rucksack and precious violin, wheeled out of the factory gates in the Harbottle family Ford.

'Not a bad run,' the CSM reflected, 'even if my wife, Rosie, will tell me I'm later than I promised. She'll be surprised to see you, though.'

'What do you mean, Sergeant Major? I thought you were dropping me at the town centre.'

'Bit late for that, lad. But it's time I asked you a second question.'

'A second question?'

'Aye. You answered the first question while we were still with Mother Brown. You told the truth when you said your name was Daniel Selby from Melbridge, didn't you?'

'Yes, that's right.'

'So now comes my second question. Who, or what, are you running away from? School or home? And let's have the truth – no ifs and buts.'

There was a pause: Danny seemed lost for an answer. Then he said, 'I think the truthful answer is both of them, CSM.'

'Uh huh?'

'The school, certainly. I don't fit there, you see. It's like being forced into a ready-made suit which is too small for you. Do you understand?'

'Aye. And what about your dad and mum in Melbridge?'

'That's different. I'm very fond of them. Only, you see, they were both (Dad especially) very keen for me to go to Highminster.'

'So they'll be angry at what you've done, eh?'

'Not exactly. But I needed time – and even distance – to explain why I couldn't stick the school any longer.'

'Right – and you're making use of your friend's invitation to stay in the Lake District? And you trusted Mother B. to find you a truck-hop to Preston? You've got some nerve.'

Bert Harbottle smiled.

'OK Danny, no more questions. Now I'll give you a bit of army advice. If you're away from headquarters on detachment, the first thing you do on reaching your destination is to give your new map reference to HQ. In this case, it's simple: Preston, Lancs, care of Mr and Mrs Harbottle in St Andrew's Road.'

A few minutes later, they drew up at a neat semi-detached house to be met by Rosie Harbottle, worried that Bert was behind schedule, but relieved to have him back, safe and sound.

'And look what I've brought with me, luv. Mrs Harbottle, meet Mr Daniel Selby of Melbridge, presently engaged in escaping from the South of England.'

Rosie Harbottle, smiling, plump, fiftyish, inspected Danny, as if she was deciding on the best cut at the butcher's.

'Come on in, Danny. Looks to me as if you could do with a decent meal.'

'Which goes for me, too,' said the Sergeant Major. 'But first, Danny and I will phone his pa and ma and give them his present location.'

He took Danny by the arm, put through a reverse charge call and spoke to Kathy.

'You won't know me, Mrs Selby, but I'm speaking from Preston in Lancashire and I have your son, Daniel, beside me. I'll leave him to do the talking, but I can assure you that he will be well cared for, and spend the night at home with me and my wife. Over to you, Danny.' The boy took over the phone.

'Hello, Mum. I've come straight up here to stay with Ratty, but Preston is further from Rydal than I realised. I'm sorry not to have told you of my plan earlier; and I've truly had a great day on the road. Mr Harbottle, the man who drove the lorry, has been brilliant. I think he'd like another word with you. So, goodnight Mum, and tell Dad I'm OK.'

11

Kathy was travelling to Preston alone. Settled in a first-class non-smoking compartment on the midday Royal Scot, she meant to sleep all the way. But that's not so easy when you are as mentally exhausted as she was. Her state of mind had not been improved by the journey from Waterloo to Euston – how she hated the smell, the noise and the bustle of London streets. Still, she was grateful to the genial taxi driver who had made it with ten minutes to spare; and grateful too that Joe had insisted on her travelling first class.

So here she was in a comfortable seat with the *Daily Mail* and *Woman's Journal* for company. Not that she looked at either. Her mind was endlessly revolving round the sequence of events which had ended with this lonely journey north to find their wayward son. It was at teatime the previous day when she first started to wonder what disaster could have overtaken Danny on his cross-country bus journey from Highminster to Melbridge. Why, in Heaven's name, couldn't he be like the rest of the boys who would be travelling home by train?

At six thirty p.m. she had been partially relieved to hear Mr Harbottle's homely Lancashire voice. But of course she was worried: and so was Joe when he returned very late from the office, tired out and in a bad mood after dealing with matters which could easily have been sorted out by Richard Fagg. Kathy was hotting up some supper for him when the next long-distance call came through. This time the caller was Martin Wrattenley, Ratty's father, speaking from Rydal. Daniel had been in touch, and he and his son proposed to drive over to Preston in the morning to collect him. Clearly Major Wrattenley was a bit mystified by Danny's decision to come to join them straight from school and his son, Peter, couldn't or wouldn't throw any light on the subject. Would Mr or Mrs Selby like to consider coming north for a few days? Danny was more than welcome to stay as long as he liked, but in the circumstances, maybe it would set their minds at rest if they could talk to the boy themselves. There was plenty of room for them all to stay.

Joe had accepted the invitation at once on behalf of Kathy and himself: an immediate visit to the Wrattenley home might be the quickest way to sort out the whole silly business. They had gone to bed prepared for an early start after Major Wrattenley had confirmed the time of train departure from Euston. 'We'll meet you at Preston,' he said, 'and have Daniel waiting for you.'

So far, so good: they were engaged as parents on the simple reclamation of an errant schoolboy. But then, this very morning at seven fifteen a.m., another phone call had reached them. Joseph had answered the call. Kathy had rushed to join him when she heard him say, 'Oh no, I can't believe it,' thinking there must be further news about Danny. In fact it was a very agitated Eleanor Grant. She apologised for ringing so early but felt she must tell Joseph at once that, during the night, Richard Fagg had been taken to Melchester for questioning by the police. 'That's all I know for sure, Joseph, but we've been suspicious about some of the people he's been entertaining at the Feathers these last few weeks. And last night, one of my regulars was telling me there was a police raid on a yacht at Abbotshaven. Drug Squad he reckons. I only hope it's all a misunderstanding, but it could be serious.'

It was years since Kathy had seen her husband look so depressed, and she understood her man well: his personal interest in Danny's education, and his anxiety about the boy's future, the affection between father and son which the father found so hard to express or demonstrate. But again and again, the business of Selby & Leadbitter seemed to stand in the way of closer family relationships.

Joe turned to her, outwardly calm. 'Well, my darling, you heard what Eleanor said. There's nothing for it. You'll have to travel north on your own. I'll get you on to the train at Melchester and then spend my day visiting the police and sorting out this wretched business of Richard Fagg. I'm terribly sorry . . .' Joe's voice was clipped and precise, but he was unable to hide his emotion completely as he kissed her goodbye.

'Dear Kathy, all the family problems seem to fall on you. Mind you travel first class now and try to get some sleep on the way. I'll ring you at seven o'clock this evening.'

Kathy's troubled mind was going round in small circles, switching from Danny to Joe and back again. She must have dozed off eventually and somewhere south of Crewe, was beset by the strangest of dreams. To her troubled mind Joseph was always 'on stage', engaged in a hopeless defensive battle against outside forces of overwhelming strength. Was he, in some nightmare sense, linked with King Arthur and his Romano–British force falling back on Cornwall and Camelot, as he had recounted to Becky and Daniel on one of those happy Port Isaac holidays, long ago? But Joe was not dressed for the part. Instead of Excalibur he was wielding a long quill pen and instead of armour he was wearing his normal grey trousers topped by a waistcoat and no jacket. It was all quite crazy.

He was surrounded by an incongruous horde of attackers, headed by Richard Fagg and with Grandma Selby and the odious Flora Pennington screaming abuse in the background. Kathy herself played no part in the drama – she seemed to be cast in the role of observer, gazing on a sort of joust being staged at some football stadium. Danny kept appearing and disappearing, surrounded by a strange bodyguard, ranging from Professor Podolski to an enormous truck driver. Each of them seemed more intent on protecting Danny than helping Joe . . .

She woke with a start as a dining-car attendant hurried along the corridor announcing that 'first luncheon is now being served.'

Practical as ever, she decided to get the puzzling dream out of her system with a plastic mug of tea and Digestive biscuits, followed by a tidy-up. Come what may, she would jolly well look her best on leaving the train at Preston. She wasn't even sure whom she would be meeting at the ticket barrier, but she would *not* look like a harassed mother searching for a prodigal son. Oh dear me, no. She looked again in her handmirror. Danny's supporters, male or female, would see what she saw, a good-looking young woman of thirty-eight, with a smile on her face and a wave in the auburn hair above wide-set bright eyes . . . pity that her lightweight navy blue skirt and jacket were last year's model: but still, she had a new neckline shirt, supported by a floppy cerise bow. Danny, if nobody else, would know she had dressed for the occasion. Resolutely, she pulled her suitcase from the rack, stuffed her papers into it, and walked along the corridor to the exit door, as the Royal Scot glided into the station, bang on time, at one fifteen.

The reception committee had assembled in good time. First to arrive had been Danny and Rosie Harbottle, the latter having given her charge a preview of the Preston town centre, the Guildhall, the Harris Museum, two churches and – best of all – a tour of the covered market. Next to appear had been Ratty who had alarmed Rosie with an ear-splitting cry across the concourse: 'Hi, Podolski, here we come.' Finally Major Wrattenley had joined the small group, tall, walking with a slight limp but unmistakably a soldier, with a military moustache and a straight back.

Kathy sized them up as she walked down the platform, but no sooner had she handed in her ticket than she was enveloped in a bearhug from her son. After this rapturous welcome, he seized her suitcase and informally introduced her to the rest of the party: 'Mum, this is Mrs Harbottle, who gave me a super meal last night – she is married to the Sergeant Major who brought me all the way to Preston in a ten-ton diesel; and this is Ratty's father, Major Wrattenley, and Ratty you know.'

Kathy did her best to thank Rosie for her kindness and ask discreetly what her son owed for his bed and breakfast. But Rosie would have none of it. 'Paid his way, he did, this morning. Insisted on tuning our piano – the things that boy of yours carries about in his rucksack – what was it, now, Danny? – a harp key, that's it, a wedge and a tuning lever – is that what you call 'em, Danny? And now the old piano's as good as new. And then he played a tune that fair had me dancing. It was lovely.' Rosie Harbottle had clearly enjoyed this break in routine.

Now she looked at the station clock and decided she must be getting on. 'But I've told Danny, Mrs Selby, he's always welcome at our home, provided he'll give us a tune. He's got our address and telephone number. I tell you, Mrs Selby, it's been a pleasure to 'ave 'im in our 'ouse – a real bit of Lancashire luck.'

Martin Wrattenley wove skilfully through the crowded Preston streets, and soon reached the M6, where to the boys' delight he really opened the throttle of the Lagonda until he reached junction 36 and the turn-off for Windermere.

'That's the end of the racetrack, Mrs Selby, but the beginning of the scenery. It's uphill all the way from now on, with the high Cumbrian fells and the road to Ullswater on your right. Soon we shall be skirting the northern extremity of Windermere and then move north to my neck of the woods. You've never been up here before? I think you'll find there's a lot to see.'

As the miles ticked away, Kathy's spirits rose. She looked at the driver's calm, intent profile: and liked what she saw. There could have been tragedy in his life, but this enchanted land seemed to have given him a calmness which was immensely reassuring. She was certain she could trust this man, a feeling strengthened as they drew up at his low-slung stone house, overlooking pastureland which ran down to the reedy fringe of Rydal Water. The man's home seemed as unshakeable as the surrounding hills.

Martin Wrattenley jumped from the car and came round to open the passenger door for Kathy, calling to the boys to tell Mrs Gibbs they were ready for food as soon as she could serve it. Then he turned to Kathy and helped her out of the car.

Thanking him, she looked first at the house, and then across the fields to the water. 'What a marvellous place. I've been feeling free as air, ever since we left the M6. Would you mind if I called you Martin?'

'Delighted,' he replied, 'provided I'm allowed to call you Kathy.'

Together they followed Daniel and Ratty into the house.

Joseph Selby's telephone call to Kathy reached her at seven o'clock precisely that evening, exactly as he had promised.

He was full of questions. 'How was the journey, Kathy? Not too exhausted? Met by Ratty's father in Preston? Coming back tomorrow? I'm so glad all is going well. I'll meet you at Melchester Station.'

One could be forgiven for thinking Joe had a list of questions which he was ticking off as Kathy's monosyllabic answers reached him.

'And Danny? Staying on with the Wrattenleys for a bit? Excellent idea. May help him to recover his bearings. Let me have a word with him.'

But first Kathy asked about the outcome of her husband's visit to Melchester police station, and the situation with the wretched Richard Fagg.

Evidently, Joe had spent most of the day getting him out of police custody. After hours of difficult negotiations, he had been granted conditional bail of £1,000, with orders to surrender his passport and report daily to Melbridge police station. 'It looks as though the idiot has got himself caught up on the edge of some drug racket, but I'll tell you more, darling, when you're back in Melbridge. All I will say at the moment is that I've been deceived by young Fagg, and I feel extremely angry with myself. Ahead of me lie press enquiries galore which will do the practice no good at all. But where's Danny?'

The boy took over. Very quickly, his sheer exuberance began to disperse his father's gloom. 'It's marvellous up here, Dad ... wish you were here ... Ratty and I are off on a full day's bike ride tomorrow. Major Wrattenley's housekeeper is making sandwiches for us ... Yes, the ride up to Preston was brilliant. Terribly lucky to get this lift with the Company Sergeant Major, that's Mr Harbottle, in his ten-ton diesel. Then I stayed the night because he had to help this man whose truck wouldn't start, and Mrs Harbottle came in with me to the station to meet Mum. Want another word with Mum? No? Well, goodnight, Dad. Love to Becky. Mum will bring the rest of the news tomorrow.' And Danny rang off.

No more phone calls reached number ten that night. The uncomplicated and efficient Becky cooked the dinner for her father, laughed about Danny's free ride to Preston and distracted him with talk about the University of Kent outside Canterbury, which had accepted her for a sociology degree course. Joseph Selby went early to bed thinking of Kathy and the children and banishing from his mind the fear of damage to his legal practice from the stupidity and – for all he knew – the criminal corruption of his employee. He'd face tomorrow when it came.

At the old stone house overlooking Rydal Water, Ratty and Daniel also retired shortly after supper, leaving Kathy and Martin talking over the coffee.

Kathy quickly pieced together Martin's background. He proved to be the second son of a peer, entitled to the prefix of 'honourable' which he never used. After Eton and Sandhurst, he had seen active service and promotion in Malaya and Korea, until his good fortune deserted him when he was wounded in Korea. Invalided out of the army, he had married and settled down to a satisfying life as a warden with the National Park authority when tragedy struck. His beautiful wife – there was a fine painting of her over the fireplace in the living-room – had died in hospital after a fatal road accident, leaving Martin with three sons to bring up. The two elder boys were both overseas, one in Australia, one in America at the Massachusetts Institute of Technology, leaving Martin to cope with Peter during the school holidays.

Martin, fully stretched in his duties as a Nature Warden, was delighted that his youngest son had a companion for the holidays. 'It's hard, Kathy, to develop local friendships when you spend your time at a faraway boarding school.' But he was also fascinated by what he had seen and heard of Peter's study mate.

How did Kathy account for Daniel's mercurial eccentric nature? Obviously, his musical gifts were exceptional. So, too, was his power to entertain others and command audiences. But why should these unusual gifts engender this sudden determination to leave Highminster? A fact which had come out if only obliquely already in the course of the evening.

Kathy had to admit she had no answer to this, and as a guest in a strange house she had not felt able to corner her son for a private inquisition. 'Danny was happy as a dayboy at Melbridge grammar school. He was very well taught – well enough to held his own at Highminster. In addition, he received inspired musical tuition – piano and singing from the organist and choirmaster at our parish church, and the violin from an extraordinary Polish emigré called Jan Podolski.'

'Ah, that explains the origin of those absurd conversations in which my son and Danny indulge.' They laughed together.

Martin thought for a moment. Then he said, 'I have a business meeting in London next week, and have incidentally arranged to

meet Roger Powell and his wife for lunch at my club as they'll be in
town at the same time. Would you mind if I made a casual reference
to Daniel's presence up here? Presumably Roger does not yet know
that Daniel is determined not to return to Highminster.'

'You seem very certain, Martin – about Danny's determination?'

'Only on the strength of what Peter has hinted. But I shall be
surprised if I don't get a clearer picture in the next few days. Boys,
you know, often find it easier to pour out their worries to strangers
than they do to their parents, I can't really think why. Danny strikes
me as a very sensitive type – opinionated certainly, but also anxious
not to hurt his parents whom he clearly holds in great affection. Boys
of his age can get very mixed up.'

Kathy was increasingly impressed by the assurance of this decisive
military man. She and Joe could hardly write to Roger Powell until
they had decided on the right direction for Danny's future education:
but she was sure Martin Wrattenley would help them.

'How I wish Joe was here,' she said. 'It really is a shame that he is
tied up with this crisis at home – and that's only the half of it. He's also
up to his eyes in complicated work for Lord Melchester.'

'Freddy Melchester? A bit after my time at Eton . . . father killed at
Alamein I seem to remember. Somebody told me he'd developed
a taste for fast cars and racehorses, but that was fifteen years
ago.'

The following morning, having left the two boys to their own devices,
Martin insisted on driving Kathy to Preston and seeing her safely on
to the eleven forty-nine London train. In the car they agreed to keep
in touch, and Kathy accepted an invitation, on behalf of Joseph and
herself, to return later in the month for a week's holiday.

On the return journey, her thoughts were far removed from those
that had troubled her going north. Now she felt refreshed, almost
light hearted. Was she under some Lakeland spell? Was she affected
by the peace of Rydal Water? Or the comfort of the Wrattenley
home? Or something linked to the people she'd met on this twenty-
four-hour visit – the carefree companionship of the boys? The
outgoing generosity of the Harbottles and their instant offer of
hospitality? Or the real concern of Martin for Danny's future
schooling? There was something very special about him.

She experienced no nightmares as she travelled south, in her half-sleeping half-waking state, the rhythm of the carriage wheels on the newly electrified line seemed to hammer out a plan for her son. Why should he not complete his 'O'-levels up north? Could he get into a good Preston school? No boarding, of course – but could Rosie and Bert Harbottle accept him as a paying guest? And after a year, should the musical world beckon, could Manchester provide the answer – Chetham's first, with its famous musical tradition, followed by the Royal Northern School of Music? She must talk it over with Joseph the moment she got home.

She came out of her daydreams as the train reached Euston. She was lucky to find a taxi and had time to phone Joe from Waterloo to meet her at Melchester. Poor man, he must be having a terribly worrying time. He needed a break more than she did. But would it be possible for him to get away? She'd never known him so preoccupied.

12

At 10 Ockenham Drive the early-morning tea ritual was in progress. Contrary to his usual custom, Joe was pouring a second cup for his wife as well as himself. Clearly he had something on his mind. He went straight to the point.

'The right school for Danny – I reckon that's our top priority today, Kathy.'

Kathy was wide awake now. 'But what about your office appointments?'

'Richard Fagg, the Drugs Squad and those confounded journalists? The whole lot can go to blazes so far as I'm concerned – or at least waste their day in attacking the stonewall defences of Leadbitter Jones.'

Here was good fighting stuff which Kathy correctly interpreted as being the prelude to some proposal.

'Come on, Joe. Out with it. You've got a plan for the day, haven't you?'

'Well yes, my dear. I've been thinking that it might be sensible for both of us to drive over to Highminster and have a preliminary chat with Roger Powell.'

The Selbys were in luck. When Joseph rang the school he was told Danny's housemaster would be free to see them at eleven o'clock. Next, Joe was in touch with the office to give old Leadbitter Jones his marching orders.

'Some family business, Mr Jones ... might take me away from Melbridge for a few days ... may I leave you to hold the fort?'

'Certainly, Mr Joseph. Any special instructions?'

'Well, you will naturally refer to Mr Withers' questions about the

89

bypass or anything to do with Lord Melchester's affairs. In other respects, I'll rely on you to act like Stonewall Jackson.'

'Meaning, Mr Joseph?'

'Briefly, let the staff know that Mr Fagg is at present on holiday, and any enquiries about him should be referred to you.'

'And how should I reply, Mr Joseph?'

'You know nothing, Mr Jones, nothing at all except that your colleague, Mr Fagg, is on leave. And so am I. Take a note of every caller's name and the time of his or her call, and record any other information that might later prove useful to the police.

'Oh, one final point ... no appointments for me for the next ten days. I'll ring you at home every evening after office hours. Good luck, Mr Jones.'

'Thank you, Mr Joseph.'

Leadbitter Jones – what a splendidly reliable chap to have in your office, Joe reflected as he and Kathy made for Highminster on that lovely July morning. Not that they found much joy in the smooth running of the Rover they had recently bought, nor in the peaceful green of the countryside. They travelled in silence with Joe at the wheel, their eyes fixed on the road ahead and their minds concerned with the housemaster's reception.

They need not have worried. Martin Wrattenley had been as good as his word and already mentioned Danny's arrival in the Lake District after his adventurous journey to Preston. He had also given Roger Powell a hint that Daniel might be aiming to get away from Highminster.

'If that proves to be the case, I shall be very sad.' There was a clear note of disappointment in the schoolmaster's voice as he spoke. 'But I've come to believe that if a boy doesn't accept the Highminster tradition, it's better to let him make the break quickly before he gets embittered.'

'And is that your advice?'

Roger Powell seemed to take a long time filling and lighting his pipe.

Then he said, 'No, Mr Selby. This is a matter for the parents to decide, not the schoolmaster. But I could quote you the cases of a yachtsman, a mountaineer and a novelist – all three of them

90

household names, who, in their memoirs, have each written most bitterly about the public schools which their parents forced them to attend for five miserable years. People sometimes speak of "horses for courses". The phrase could equally be applied to schools and schoolboys.'

Roger Powell paused before making his point more clearly.

'Your son, Mr and Mrs Selby, might in my view come into the same category as those three famous men. Like them, you see, he is in a very real sense a non-conformist. Oh, I don't use the phrase in a religious sense, although . . .'

'Although what, Mr Powell?' Joseph Selby was always quick to challenge a hesitant witness.

'Ah, you question my hesitation, and quite right, too. I was just remembering a tale told out of school about your son. The story goes that our chaplain was looking for confirmation candidates in Daniel's age group. He was getting a routine C of E acceptance rate until Daniel asked for the chaplain's views on the Plymouth Brethren and their doctrines. Chaplain was caught off guard, so to speak, and before he could recover his balance received another body blow. According to my informant in the senior common room, your son then went on to say that, after a close study of the textbook on comparative religion which had been prescribed by the chaplain for RI, he and some of his friends had opted in favour of Zen Buddhism! Oh dear, oh dear. A good man our chaplain, but a trifle short on humour.'

The three of them were laughing when Diana Powell entered the room with coffee and biscuits, and the talk became more general. After the success of her party for the headmaster and the fun of accompanying Daniel in the Mozart violin sonata, Diana was sure that in due course the boy would win international fame as a violinist and fill the concert halls of the world's capital cities.

But Roger had other ideas.

'You may be right about Daniel's future, my dear, but there are other exciting scenarios which might suit him equally well. I can envisage him, for instance, in a semi-political role, persuading all sorts of men and women to give up their most cherished beliefs in favour of something he advocates. I can see him also as a flamboyant

91

Don Quixote tilting at the most sacred "windmills" of the Establishment. But, Heavens alive, Daniel's only fifteen ... shouldn't we give him a few years in which to make up his own mind?'

As the Selbys took their leave, Joe looked back regretfully at the spacious Victorian architecture of Highminster School, which twelve months earlier had seemed so attractive. Kathy sensed his disappointment: he had hoped for so much from Highminster and would hate to see his master plan for Danny miscarry.

Both the Powells saw them to their car. 'Please be assured, Mr and Mrs Selby, that I retain the very highest regard for your son's character and ability,' Roger Powell assured them. 'Indeed, I have put my assessment in writing just in case it is some use to you if you decide Daniel should move elsewhere.'

With that, Roger handed an envelope to Joe. While Joe was adjusting his seatbelt, Diana leant into the car and impulsively kissed Kathy.

'Don't worry too much, my dear, about your Danny. I'm sure he will reach the summit, whichever mountain he chooses to climb, and Roger and I will watch his progress with a very personal interest. For both of us it is "au revoir" – not "goodbye".'

Somehow, the sky seemed clearer than on the outward journey. The sun shone more brightly over the rolling hills and pastureland of southern England as the new car purred its way back to Melbridge.

The next step was clear enough – a journey north for both of them and an effort to get a positive response from Danny. By the time they reached Melbridge, a clear strategy had been established.

Joe would stay in the house and make phone calls. Kathy would show herself in the town. In Joe's words, 'In a small place like Melbridge, it's better to keep your friends informed when you are making some unusual move. Otherwise "no news" becomes "mystery" and "mystery" begets "rumour".'

Walking across the Close to stock up the fridge for Becky in the East Street shops, Kathy had three fortunate encounters: with John Lucas and Harry Leng near the school and Edward Baynes walking from the church to the vicarage in Southside. To all of them she told the same story: 'Off for a few days' holiday in the Lake District before picking up Danny in Rydal.'

Before going to bed, Kathy and Joe again studied Roger Powell's reference for their son.

Concerning Daniel Selby of Melbridge
(an assessment by Mr Roger Powell MA, Highminster School)

I consider Daniel to be one of the most interesting characters to come under my care during my twenty-five years as a teacher – the last fifteen at Highminster School.

1. Aged fifteen years two months, this boy is, in physical terms, a 'late developer' but mentally he is well in advance of his age.

2. Before he reached Highminster with a music scholarship, he was known to have exceptional gifts: as a pianist with a sensitive approach to the classical composers and an ability to pick out and harmonise any 'pop' hit that attracted his friends; as a violinist with exceptional technique, acquired in private tuition from an ex-patriate Polish professor of music; and vocally, as a treble soloist with a marvellous purity of pitch (his voice is now gradually descending to the lower register).

3. At Highminster, it was necessary to upgrade him to join the scholarship class of his year; and he has surpassed his peers in English and history. He possesses a gift for writing sonorous English and for memorising poetry; and in history he displays a deep understanding of the motives and movements behind historical change. His imagination, as well as his comprehension, has clearly been aroused by teachers at his previous school in Melbridge.

4. He also has the gifts of a 'showman'. Whenever he comes 'on stage', he seems to move into a higher gear so that he not only engages the audience's close attention but also stirs their imagination.

   He seems unconscious of this gift. It certainly has not 'turned his head': nor has it made him bumptious or conceited. On the contrary, he remains extremely modest, is

93

well liked by the other boys and has a lively sense of humour.

I commend him to all who may be involved in his further education.
Roger Powell, Highminster, 1976

From Edward Baynes' Diary, 1976

As I was crossing the Close on my way to the vicarage this afternoon I met Kathy Selby returning from the East Street shops. She stopped to tell me that she and Joe were off to the Lake District for a short holiday, so they wouldn't be in church on Sunday evening. I was delighted to hear her news and told her it was high time Joe took a break from his worries over Richard Fagg and I was reasonably sure that his capable partners in the golf club venture would not be lost without him.

But Kathy didn't fool me. I knew, as did one or two other people in Melbridge, of Danny's lorry-hopping departure from Highminster. It was young Daniel, without a doubt, who had dictated his parents' holiday location. And I fell to wondering from what ancestral source had this boy drawn his musical inspiration.

Whether one measured his genius by the versatility of his performance at Podolski's grammar school concert, or by the eccentricities of his first year at Highminster, one fact is indisputable: Daniel Selby will never conform to the standards on which his parents' lives are based. However great their mutual love and understanding, Danny will choose his own way in life.

So what of Becky? Unlike her brother, she conforms easily enough. Whenever I meet her I am reminded of her mother at the same age. It won't be long before she leaves Ockenham Drive to set up her own home.

But what common interest do Joe and Kathy share, apart from love of their children? If Joe continues to be totally

94

absorbed in his legal practice, what will Kathy do with her life? She is still a very attractive young woman. But as she told me of her forthcoming holiday with Joe, I sensed a sort of desperation in her voice – and it was not entirely concerned with Danny's future.

13

The Clansman left Euston on time at nine thirty-five, heading for the North. Joe immersed himself in *The Economist*'s leading article. Sitting opposite him Kathy read Roger Powell's assessment of their gifted but awkward 'non-conformist' son for the third time before replacing it in her handbag. Then she sat back, her eyes shut and her mind full of speculation. From whom, she asked herself, did Danny inherit these qualities which again and again marked him as different? Different not only from other boys but different from his own sister, the pretty, predictable, protective Becky. Strange, very strange. She looked sleepily across at her husband. And how, she wondered, would the schoolmaster assess her Joe? Kathy began to enumerate his qualities. Discreet, honourable, efficient without a doubt. Clever, certainly. Single-minded in purpose – single-minded to a fault, she added wistfully. Too self-disciplined to show affection or make friends easily . . . Still, whatever other people thought, she knew that, deep down, Joe was fired by a great love for his family. After all, it was concern for Danny that had torn him from his blessed office when the practice was facing a series of crises, each of which demanded his presence.

With her eyes half-closed, she might well have resumed her catalogue of Joe's qualities – his good looks, for instance, and his physical courage. But she was suddenly wide awake, conscious of the great express slowing down. She looked out of the window. Sure enough, the Clansman was on the through line clearing Rugby station and Kathy's mind switched back to Danny as the station's name reminded her of his uncensored criticism of the 'barbaric' game born in this place. She smiled at the memory. A non-conformist was he? A heretic? Well, so were other great men, if Roger Powell was to be believed. And she was honest enough to admit she felt a large measure of sympathy with Danny's reaction to the class-conscious types he associated with Highminster. Anyway, she wouldn't swap Danny for all the tea in China.

Point was given to the outworn cliché by the arrival of the dining-car attendant with tea and biscuits. Joe emerged from a perusal of the *Financial Times* which had taken the place of *The Economist*, paid for the tea, and surprised Kathy by asking whether she'd given any further thought to taking up golf.

'Golf, Joe?'

Joe's self-deprecatory smile conceded that in their present circumstances his question was something of a *non sequitur*. But an article in the *Financial Times* on the cost of building a golf course had brought the subject back to the front of his mind.

'It also confirms Bob Withers' belief that a golf course for Melchester, carved out of the land on the Melchester side of the new bypass, could prove profitable.'

'So you're really serious?'

'Yes, indeed . . . I'm currently engaged in forming a company, to be called Melbridge Golf Club: and a golf course architect has already been approached.'

'And how much is it all going to cost?'

'Well, that's where this newspaper article gives a bit of guidance. It's very precise in its costings. I've jotted it all down and will compare the figures with Bob's estimates as soon as I get back to Melbridge.'

'So what are you looking for?'

'On present values, I put the total cost at £500,000.'

Joe rapidly scanned his notes:

a) Land for 18-hole course and practice ground (course to measure 6,500 to 7,000 yards) will require 150 acres at £250 per acre, say £40,000

b) Architect £5,000

c) Construction:

18 greens at £10,000	£180,000
18 tees at £4,000	72,000
fairways, bunkers	35,000

d) Drainage and irrigation	50,000
e) Mechanical equipment	80,000
f) Staff of 4, allow	41,000 p.a.

'Yes, I think we can get by on £500,000.'

'And who provides the cash, Joe?'

'Ah, that's the next big question. Bob Withers understands that Lord Melchester and his brother-in-law may have ideas, but I wonder whether we cannot find fifty people to contribute £10,000 each, in return for life membership.'

'And you'll be one of the first life members, Joe?'

'Well, why not, my dear? In five years' time it might prove a very good investment.'

Joe pocketed his neatly written notes, looked at his watch and lifted the two suitcases down from the luggage rack. He smiled reassuringly at Kathy. 'No more golf today, Kathy. It's time to concentrate on Daniel's future. Let's hope it also proves a good investment.'

The boy was easily spotted, wearing an open-necked shirt, tanned by the sun, waving to them beside the ticket collector. In a moment he was hugging them both, so full of news that words seemed to stumble over each other.

'Mum, Dad, great to see you ... hotel's just round the corner, no need for a taxi ... I've checked your booking, everything OK ... message waiting for Dad at reception ... It's brilliant up here ... but it's great to see you ... The Major drove me to Windermere, then I took the train, changing at Oxenholme ... knew I'd be early, so I rang Rosie (you know, Mrs Harbottle), took her for a cup of tea here at the station–' Danny was still chatting away as they checked in at their hotel.

Before inspecting their room Joe opened the note handed him by the reception clerk. It asked Mr Selby from Melbridge to confirm he could keep a four p.m. appointment with a firm of solicitors in Winckley Square. The writer hoped to supply Mr Selby with the advice he required.

'So far, so good,' said Joe as he returned from the call box with a rather smug smile on his face; and added for Kathy's benefit, 'Just a little private hunch, my dear: I'll tell you more later. But first let's see about lunch.'

* * *

Preston's old coaching inn, the Bull and Royal, might lack some of the latest refinements of the American hotel industry, but on this July day in 1976 it provided its clientele with an excellent menu. As soon as the family had settled for the cold salmon, Joe brought the conversation back to the problem of Danny's schooling.

There appeared, he said in his lawyer-logical style, to be three possibilities: first, to continue at Highminster as Roger Powell hoped; secondly to return to Melbridge where Danny would be sure of a warm welcome from John Lucas and first-class tuition in piano and violin from Harry Leng and the Professor; or thirdly, to find a school, as yet unidentified, which might be closer to the factory floor than the Highminster tradition. 'I think that's about the size of it, Danny. How do you see it?'

The boy was silent for a moment, clearly embarrassed by a desire not to upset his parents; but gradually the words came together.

'I'm terribly sorry but, honestly, Highminster is simply not my scene ... it's difficult to explain ... you see, most of the people there assume that birth and money give them a sort of natural right to govern England, if not the world ... Dad, I know I'm exaggerating the case ... Let me put it another way. Of the 650 boys at Highminster, hardly one of them comes from Preston or Blackburn or places where things are made ... Old Podolski would say that when they sing Parry's "Jerusalem" they haven't a clue as to what Blake was writing about.' The boy was getting worked up. 'Yes, and at the end of term, those whopping great cars that collect them – Rolls, Mercedes, Saab, you name it – paid for by their fathers' companies ... See what I mean? It sort of gets you down: and a few real people, like the Powells or Ratty and his father, aren't strong enough to buck the system ... Sorry to seem so critical, but ...'

Danny returned gratefully to his salmon and new potatoes. Kathy was lost for words. She'd never heard her son so articulate, and never felt any such bitterness during her happy schooldays at Melchester High. Nor did Joe attempt to argue the case. Perhaps he recalled his own sense of outrage when his father had stopped him from sitting for an Oxford scholarship.

'Fair enough, Danny,' he said. 'You've made your point. So what about a return to Melbridge?'

'Well, it's certainly a possibility,' the boy admitted. 'But surely you and Mum decided against it when you entered me for the Highminster music scholarship. Do you want to go back to square one?'

'So you'd prefer to try something new – different – unknown?'

'Well, not exactly, Dad. What about Preston? Mind you, I don't know much about the schools up here. But Rosie says they've got some good ones. And Rosie says that if I come up here she'll let me stay in her spare room . . . she told me so this morning over our cup of tea . . . I'm sure you'll like her, Dad. Mum likes her, don't you, Mum?'

Was her so tentative speculation looking like coming true? Kathy looked at Joe and they smiled acceptance. The boy's reasoning had drawn them way beyond their own experience or that of their Melbridge friends. They had travelled further than the 250-odd miles between Preston and Melbridge, but not beyond the horizon of their imagination.

Accepting the boy's case, Joe knew what to do next. He suggested that Daniel and Kathy should explore the town, and join him again at the Bull and Royal in time for dinner. Meanwhile he would keep his appointment in Winckley Square.

'No,' he said to Kathy. 'This appointment has no connection with Selby & Leadbitter. I'm just following a hunch which caused me to make some long-distance calls yesterday afternoon after our return from Highminster. I hope to return from this meeting with a clear picture of the best Preston school for our Danny.'

'So you knew in advance the way the boy's mind was moving?'

'Well, not exactly, my dear. But listening to Roger Powell, I felt sure he thought a complete change of scene was the best way forward for Danny. The man I shall be seeing is not only the senior partner in a leading firm of Preston solicitors but also a borough councillor with a special interest in educational policy.'

When the family reassembled, Joe reported he anticipated no difficulty in getting Danny enrolled in Ashton High School where he would take his 'O'-levels. 'The school has a fine record according to my informant; and it's on the Blackpool side of the town, so reasonably close to the Harbottles' home. I also learnt that my legal friend is a member of the congregation at St John the Baptist. That's the parish church and he says it has a fine musical tradition. We might follow this up with Ted Baynes when we get home. The Law,' Joe added rather pompously, 'is not the only profession whose members give mutual aid to their professional colleagues.'

While the solicitors were in conference, Danny had taken his mother for a walk in the gardens beside the Ribble and returned past the Harbottles' semi where they had surprised Rosie weeding between her roses in the front garden.

Tea inevitably followed in a spotlessly kept kitchen, and with it the assurance that if Mr and Mrs Selby let Danny have his way, she and Mr Harbottle would make their spare room available. 'Our two boys are overseas now, one in Sydney and one in British Columbia, and both with good jobs. But in their schooldays we saw to it that they always got there in time, with their homework properly completed.'

Who would doubt it? Kathy's spirits rose. Her conventional Melbridge world might have been turned upside down, but she never doubted that her son would be safe under the care of this kindly, smiling Lancashire woman. Generous by nature and ample in form, Rosie was one of those people you would trust to the ends of the earth. The same standard would hold, she was sure, with the 'super' Sergeant Major, described in such glowing terms by Danny. The boy had surely struck lucky. Let's follow the advice to every competitor and play on our luck, she said to herself.

Next morning they called on the headmaster at Ashton High School and completed formalities for Danny's entry in September. The decision had been taken, the deed was done and now, thought Kathy, they could look forward to the reward of a few carefree days together as a family. She felt her spirits lift at the prospect and on the way to the station even bought herself some smart blue slacks in a summer sale.

The Wrattenleys, father and son, met the local train at Windermere and all seemed set for an idyllic holiday. A trip to spot deer in the woods above Ambleside was already being considered as the party unloaded their suitcases at the house overlooking Rydal Water. But they were met by Mrs Gibbs, the housekeeper, with disturbing news. She had received three telephone calls for Mr Selby. One from a Mr Fagg, the second from a Mr Jones and a third from the Melchester police. She had taken note of their telephone numbers and each had asked Mr Selby to call back at his earliest convenience. Mr Fagg, in particular, sounded more than a little agitated.

14

Kathy was furious. She knew exactly what Joe's reaction would be. He'd be off back to Melbridge at the crack of dawn, murmuring words that brought no comfort – 'nothing for it, my dear . . . so sorry . . . duty and all that . . .'

She was crying with frustration as she rushed upstairs to the twin-bedded guest room which she had found so pleasing on her previous visit. But today she did not pause at the window for a sight of the peace of Rydal Water. She saw nothing of the contrasting shades of green picked out by the evening sun in the low ground surrounding the reed-fringed lake; nor the lengthening shadows of the hills beyond. She kicked off her shoes and lay sprawled across the white bedspread, her face buried in the pillow. It's doubtful if she even knew that Joe had entered the room, tidied away the shoes and laid the other bedcover over her.

Her mind was seething with self-pity. On the train and overnight in Preston, she and Joe had briefly enjoyed their old companionship as they shared the problem of Danny's schooling. She had even been able to laugh at the intrusion of those golf course statistics. But did she really know what Joe considered his real priorities? Did the family take second place to the family practice when the chips were down?

Inevitably questions about Joe's preoccupations turned into self-questioning. So she'd become, had she, no more to Joe than an efficient housekeeper like the excellent Mrs Gibbs downstairs? And the sexual attraction she'd enjoyed in their early years together had lapsed – let's face it – into a routine observance which gave neither of them any deep pleasure. And what was there to take its place?

Nothing. Nothing at all, except Becky and Danny who were already feeling their way forward to independence.

After a time she calmed down, but she was in no mood to join the others for an evening meal. Pleading a headache and exhaustion from the activities of the last few days, she let Joe bring her some clear soup and chicken sandwiches and was asleep or pretending to be by the time Joe came to bed. She was still sleeping when, early next morning, he crept quietly out of their room en route for Melbridge and the highly charged problem of Richard Fagg.

She woke to the sound of curtains being drawn and the smell of freshly brewed coffee. She noted bleakly that Joe had already left. The homely voice of Mrs Gibbs was asking whether she would prefer her breakfast at the table by the window or to have it served in bed on the tray. 'A lovely morning, madam, and the weatherman promises a fine day.'

A few moments later, the boys burst into the room to find Kathy looking out across the lake before sitting down to grapefruit, coffee, fresh rolls and a choice of home-made marmalade or local honey.

'Mrs Gibbs makes those rolls herself,' said Danny, eyeing the tray in front of his mother. 'That's right, isn't it, Ratty?'

'And most of the bread too,' Peter agreed. 'Not to mention the scones and a special sort of fruit cake which Father often takes with him on his tours of inspection. Actually he's away today on business in Penrith.'

'What are you going to do today, Mum? Mrs Gibbs says she'll lend you her bike, if you'd like to join us. We've an appointment with old Bill.'

'Mr Bailey, if you don't mind, Podolski.' Both boys burst out laughing and Danny began to explain. Mr Bailey, it transpired, was a cabinet-maker, very much on his dignity, a superb craftsman who now lived in some old stable attached to a farm on the road to Keswick. Major Wrattenley, who spent much of his time in a well-equipped wood workshop at the back of the house, had learnt new skills from William Bailey and had asked the boys to see how the old recluse was faring.

They had been once and were now planning a second visit at Mr Bailey's invitation.

'His place is full of ingenious gadgets and fabulous furniture he's designed and built himself.' Danny was loud in his praise. 'And he's got a silver trophy he won years ago at the Grasmere Games. And a piano. But the best bit is he specialises in repairing old violins.

'And he's told Danny he'll show him how to use the special tools you need for the job,' put in Ratty. 'If Danny puts up a good show on Mr Bailey's piano, he's been promised a rat's tail file that's going spare. Jolly decent of the old boy, don't you think?'

The boys' invitation to join their expedition was genuine enough and Kathy could not help but feel warmed by it. But she had the good sense to realise that they – and probably Mr Bailey too – would have a happier day if she was not included in the party.

She finished her breakfast and dressed in time to wave them off, their bicycles carrying an ample packed lunch, and including one of Mrs Gibbs' special fruit cakes for old William.

The bubbling enthusiasm of the two boys acted like a tonic to Kathy and, if any trace of the previous evening's despair lingered in her mind, it melted away under the warmth of the summer sun. Let Joseph Selby toil away, if he must, at his legal chores in Melbridge. She was going to enjoy to the full her days in this lovely corner of England.

Carefree, she decided to walk the few miles into Grasmere. She'd buy the statutory holiday postcards for her family at Holmesdale, for her neighbours in Ockenham Drive, and, of course, for Grandmother Selby even though the poor old lady was unlikely to thank her for the thought. Yes, she'd write them, post them, and perhaps 'do' the obligatory visit to Dove Cottage and pick up the Wordsworth trail. Not her favourite poet, she had to admit, but still he had his moments . . .

A haze of schoolroom memories began to steal over her as she walked along the Grasmere road. Well, it was hardly possible to wander 'lonely as a cloud' any more in Grasmere, and it was the wrong time of year for, what was it – yes – 'A host of golden daffodils/Beside the lake, beneath the trees/Fluttering and dancing on the breeze.'

But she found the cottage, as well as the humble graves of William and his Mary in the crowded churchyard, and the place, she sensed, was alive with those who had loved this spot long ago – the Wordsworths and Coleridge and their friends, famous and unknown.

In the little town a baker sold her freshly made sandwiches which she took down to the lakeside to eat. There she wrote her postcards and, duty done, lay back on a grassy slope from which she could gaze across the water.

A panorama of glorious contrasts opened out before her eyes: the hills and rocky outcrops, the wooded slopes, a flock of sheep moving towards fresh pastures under the control of a dog obeying the rough voice and imperious whistle of a Cumbrian shepherd. Soon she fell asleep and time stood still.

Hours later, she awoke to the same scene, except that the colouring had subtly changed in the afternoon sun, and the shepherd and his flock had passed beyond her view. Her imagination repeopled the place with the Wordsworth children at play, Dorothy Wordsworth writing, and she could surely see on that fell over there young athletes grappling their way to the summit and descending at breakneck speed as they leaped from rock to rock? And surely the young man racing towards the winning post and the cheering crowd must be young William Bailey, the cabinet-maker, who still polishes the silver trophy he had won as a youth at the Grasmere Games.

Kathy shut and opened her eyes, shaking herself free of the past. The phantoms vanished as the sun sank slowly behind the western skyline. Resolute and relaxed, she picked her way along the field path leading back to Rydal and the Wrattenley home.

At the point where the track joined the metalled road which ran beside the small stretch of water, she felt a new vigour assail her, a sort of exhilaration which made a mockery of her thirty-eight years. It must be the effect of the Lakeland air, she supposed, as she covered the final four hundred yards to Martin's house. Of one thing she was certain. Tonight she would do full justice to Mrs Gibbs' ample provisions for the family.

15

That night Mrs Gibbs served a most excellent dinner – roast chicken with bread sauce, courgettes and new potatoes from the garden, followed by late crop raspberries and cream.

'When the Major gets back from his monthly meetings in Penrith he needs a good meal,' she had confided to Kathy. 'Nothing fancy, you understand, he prefers old-fashioned English dishes – but a good meal helps when you're tired. And he *does* get bored, does the Major, with these long-winded committees. The business, he will tell you, could all be settled in ten minutes if the army was in charge. But he's a very patient man, bless him. Reckon he sees himself as an umpire keeping the peace between all the do-gooders and the developers, to make sure they don't break the Park rules.'

'And the raspberries, Mrs Gibbs?'

'Aye, they're something a bit special,' Mrs Gibbs conceded. 'Grown by my brother who has a wife and family in the village, and looks after our garden here.'

The housekeeper bustled away to the kitchen, remarking as she went that she'd be surprised to see any raspberries left after them two boys had taken their pick.

At dinner the talk turned first to the boys' visit to Mr Bailey.

'Fantastic what he's made of those stables, Mum – everything centred on the stable yard: wood storage and workshop on one side, the bit where he lives on the other.'

Peter took up the story. 'And he's not a bit what you expect for a hermit,' he said. 'I mean nothing like an Old Testament prophet with a long beard. He's neat and clean-shaven, with strange sort of penetrating eyes . . .'

'That's about right,' Martin broke in to the boy's duet. 'Harry is a born fellsman with the eyes of a mountaineer, steel blue like Smythe or Shipton.'

'And what did you do there?'

'Well, there was "an incident".' Peter took up the story again with a hoot of laughter. 'Danny saw a violin the old man had been repairing and twanged a string. Mr Bailey was very angry. To put it mildly he was not amused.'

'Don't know why I did it,' confessed Danny.

'It was not a bit funny at the time. But Peter brought him back into good humour by unpacking the grub and Mrs Gibbs' fruit cake. We ate the lot in the stable yard sitting on garden chairs designed by the old man. I think it was Mrs Gibbs' cake did the trick – calmed him down, so to speak . . .'

'Bunkum,' Peter broke in. 'It was Danny's "double Podolski" that worked the miracle. Danny, you see, was running through some Chopin on Mr Bailey's piano, like he promised on our last visit and I was getting a brew on in the kitchen with the old boy, and I told him that Danny's first love was the violin. So he was allowed to have a go. You should have seen the old man's face. You could tell he was impressed because not only did he give Danny the set of tools for mending violins, Mrs Selby, but he told him he'd be welcome as an apprentice when he leaves school. What d'you say to that?'

Peter was laughing as he concluded the story of Danny's 'double Podolski', but Martin Wrattenley, perhaps sensing Danny's embarrassment, took Mr Bailey's proposition more seriously.

'Good for you, Danny,' he said. 'I fancy your parents may have some views on what you do with yourself after your 'O'-levels. But still, you never can tell. If I were you, I'd store old William's offer in the back of my mind. There are worse jobs in life, you know, than making beautiful furniture and bringing old violins back to life.'

Again and again, through the meal, Kathy found her eyes returning to Martin's strong features – the ascetic cheekbones, the neat moustache, the serious expression relieved by questing eyes and the hint of a smile as he listened to the boys' chatter. Clearly, he enjoyed a close rapport with this youngest son he had brought up single-handed for fourteen years since his wife's tragic death. But his interest in Daniel was also apparent. Was it relief perhaps, that

Peter's rather solitary holidays from Highminster had been transformed by Danny's companionship? Or were his thoughts more
complex? Sometimes it seemed to Kathy as if Martin was probing the
boy's future, wondering how his musical gifts might fit in with his
declared egalitarian principles.

Martin turned to her, jerking her out of her private speculations.

'Well, Kathy, how would you like to spend tomorrow? Any special
ideas?'

Caught by surprise, Kathy said she'd be happy to fit in with any
plan the others had in mind, and found herself faced with two
possibilities – join Peter and Daniel who wanted to hire a boat on
Coniston, or accompany Martin on a trip to the hills beyond
Ambleside where poachers or vandals were said to be disturbing the
deer.

'The trouble with Peter and Daniel,' said Martin, 'is that they're
determined to visit as many places as possible in the days they have
together. They're a bit like those English tourists who boast of the
number of European frontiers they have crossed in the course of a
fortnight's holiday.'

Whatever their motives, Kathy was clear as to her preference.

'Better, I'd say, to leave a coxless pair to steer their own course.
Anyway, I don't want my new peacock-blue slacks splashed by
amateur oarsmen. But don't worry about me. I'll be happy to be on
my own, provided you can dump me at a suitable rendezvous.'

'No problem.' Martin was looking at his OS map. 'We're all
heading in the same direction, so we take the Land-Rover, load the
boys' bikes as usual, drop them at the lakeside to hire a boat and find
some food. Then you and I, Kathy, establish main headquarters at
some place . . .' He paused for a moment looking at his map. 'Yes,
here we are . . . the old Roman camp just above Windermere. It's
marked as Borran's Field. I'll leave you there to guard Mrs Gibbs'
picnic basket, while I move off to Ambleside to keep my date with the
police.'

'Hey, wait a minute,' Kathy was positive. 'Not so fast, please. I
don't feel like spending the day as a resident "tea lady". Some
exercise, Martin, is essential. Your housekeeper's holiday diet,
though delectable, holds dangers for a woman accustomed to
Melbridge's more meagre rations.'

Martin began to laugh. 'Fair enough,' he said, looking first at Kathy's trim figure and then at the map.

'Let's try again. Right, here's what we do – leave the picnic with the National Trust office at Borran's Field, before carting the boys and their bikes down to Coniston. Then I'll show you the view from Jenkins Crag. On a clear day it's a sight worth seeing and it's reasonably close to Ambleside where I'm due to meet the police. I'll leave you with the OS map to make your own way in your own time to reach the Roman camp. I'll rejoin you as soon as I can.

'Whatever we do, we all reach Borran's Field by four o'clock in time for tea and leave an hour later for Rydal and a barbecue evening. It's Mrs Gibbs' day off, but she'll leave everything we need in the kitchen.'

And so it was arranged. The following morning, the boys and their bikes were offloaded at the lakeside and Martin and Kathy drove back to Ambleside where they parked the car and under a cloudless sky set off on a well-marked track along the lower slope of Wansfell. The point known as Jenkins Crag proved to be blessedly clear of tourists and Kathy suddenly felt an uncanny sense of kinship with the fabulous panorama opening before her. She quickly spotted the statuesque Langdale Pikes, erect as sentinels on eternal watch. Beyond them in the distance towered the high peaks – Sca Fell, Helvellyn, Skiddaw – their romantic names so often bandied about by Martin and the boys. To the north-west the Kirkstone Pass was threading its way towards Keswick, while below her the Rothay stream, which she had earlier encountered by Wordsworth's cottage, was meandering through a green valley towards its outlet in Windermere.

She felt an overpowering impulse to hug the man beside her in gratitude for his kindness in bringing such beauty to her eyes: but Martin was already consulting his watch.

'Mustn't keep the police waiting.' He handed over a small packet marked 'Mrs S. lunch'. 'And here's my map to guide you to Borran's Field. I'll try to be back with you by three o'clock ... goodbye for now...' Kathy watched him striding down the path without a backward glance.

Left to herself, she enjoyed her packed lunch at Jenkins Crag, but found her way to Borran's Field long before Martin returned from his business with the police. She was in fact sitting in the area marked 'Praetorium', dreamily peopling it with centurions and conscript Roman legionnaires, when the spell was broken by Martin's arrival.

She would like to have known why a Roman general – hadn't Martin named him Agricola? – should have set up so large a supply base in this mountainous corner of England. But such thoughts were interrupted by the arrival of the two boys, exhausted and hungry, clamouring for food.

They seemed to have enjoyed their day on Coniston Water, judging by the snatches of conversation she picked up as they demolished Mrs Gibbs' picnic. 'Great day . . . had a race with two other blokes . . . no, they won . . . we couldn't keep straight . . . good fun, though . . . any more tea, Mum? . . . had to push our bikes most of the way up here . . .'

Peter and Danny were still talking of their boating adventures as the Land-Rover took the party back to Rydal and the promised barbecue, where Martin was in his element grilling the sausages, chops and tomatoes.

They continued talking on the terrace until the sun set over Rydal Water. But as they entered the house, Kathy and her son were sadly aware that there was only one more day left to their Lakeland holiday. However, Martin was now free of appointments and would be taking the next day off. Indeed, he had already agreed to transport the boys and their bikes to Keswick where they were picking up some films and intending to make a further call on William Bailey on their way home. So would Kathy like to take the opportunity of making a tour of the more distant lakes?

No? The lady would prefer another walk? In that case, he would conduct her back from Keswick and they would make a sharp climb to a point from which they could look across to Friar's Crag and survey Derwent Water in all its beauty. Given fine weather, that was a sight she must not miss, Martin was most insistent. Then, assuming the fine weather held, they would take a late lunch in Langdale.

There was still no word from Melbridge. This did not surprise Kathy. Joe would only call her when he had something positive to report. Meanwhile, let her give thanks for a lovely day.

She was already settling down to sleep when a slight figure in

111

pyjamas appeared at her door. Seeing his mother was awake, Danny perched himself on the side of her bed, kissed her lightly on the forehead and suddenly blurted out, 'Mum, shall I tell you something? Ratty thinks you're absolutely brilliant. Honest, he told me so himself. You see, he never knew his own mother and you make him see what he's missed. Not that he's jealous – he's not that sort – but that beautiful painting downstairs which means so much to Major Wrattenley leaves him sort of cold if you see what I mean . . . like a statue, I suppose, which won't come alive.'

The tousle-haired bespectacled boy did not expect or wait for an answer. Almost abruptly, he kissed her again and rose from the bed. The last Kathy heard of her son that night was the sound of his slippered feet padding along the uncarpeted landing to his friend's room. She couldn't think why, but there were tears in her eyes as she turned off the light.

16

Martin and Kathy were sitting side by side, looking down on Derwent Water. They were resting on the high ground which borders one side of the lake, after climbing up a grassy track from the Keswick road where they had parked the car. Far below them, the lake water was sparkling in the morning sunshine. Derwent Water was in its most peaceful mood, in colourful contrast to the threatening contours of the high peaks to the north and east. The rich variety of the landscape was truly startling to a woman brought up amid the rolling farmlands and little woods and slopes of southern England. The country through which they had driven that morning, between Keswick and Ambleside, was dominated by tough volcanic rock with craggy profiles like Sca Fell or the Langdales – a perfect training ground for mountaineers. And the day before the landscape to the south was transformed into the softer wooded hills round Coniston and Windermere. You look around you, thought Kathy, and you take your choice. 'It's fabulous ... pure magic,' she murmured half to herself.

Somewhere a church clock struck twelve, bringing them back to the present with a jerk.

'My goodness, Kathy, it's time to make a move if we're to reach Langdale while the sun is high.' Martin jumped to his feet, took hold of her hands and pulled her up.

'I know a spot where we can make the most of Mrs Gibbs' picnic, but it means another climb first.'

'Something special about the rations, Martin? You sound a bit mysterious.'

'No, it's just that I like to humour this housekeeper of mine. From

113

time to time she recalls her early training as a parlourmaid in some stately mansion in Gloucestershire, and puts her training to good use if she approves of the company involved, as she certainly does in the case of you and Danny. So, when she talks about "something special" for the last day of Mrs Selby's holiday – and a bottle of wine to go with it – I'm full of expectation.'

As they headed for Langdale in the Land-Rover, Kathy posed the question she had meant to ask her companion yesterday at Borran's Field about why the Roman soldiers decided to build a great supply base near Windermere.

'The Romans, Kathy? I reckon Peter and Daniel are better informed than I am. In my schooldays we leapt from Julius Caesar 55 BC to the Norman Conquest AD 1066. And a hell of a lot can happen in eleven hundred years. All I know is that the Romans governed this island for over four hundred years which is nearly three times as long as we ruled India.'

'And then,' added Kathy triumphantly, recalling family holidays in Cornwall long ago, 'a brilliant general whom we know as King Arthur, led his people westwards, conducting a brilliant rearguard action against the hordes of German invaders. At least, that's what Joe told the children,' she added, slightly annoyed with herself for letting Joe intrude into the conversation.

'Joe's probably right,' Martin conceded. 'It was a bit different up here mind, because of the Vikings. All those place names up here ending in "thwaite" and "side" are Norse in origin.'

'And as all these invaders married the local girls, you might say we're a race of mongrels?'

'Yes, I suppose so, though I think the Cumbrians, like the Cornish and the Welsh, might claim to be "true Brits"!'

'Not to worry, Martin, personally I'm rather fond of mongrels.'

The front-seat conversation petered out as they entered Langdale and Martin wheeled left off the metalled road and proceeded for a hundred yards up a wide track marked 'public footpath', to park at a point where the track became a single-file footpath.

'This is where we dismount and use our feet,' he said, pulling two rucksacks and a couple of sticks out of the car. He harnessed the lighter load on Kathy's back, handed her one of the sticks, and confidently led the way up a rough path, criss-crossed by little streams.

They climbed steadily, but after sticking to the public footpath for about a mile, Martin turned off the track, beating a way through the bracken and heading towards a rock projecting from the hillside. Rounding it, they reached a small, grassy patch of level ground.

'How's that for a picnic site?' Martin spoke with the confidence of an estate agent extolling an attractive property to a prospective buyer. 'Uninterrupted view of the valley, the Great Langdale Pike to be seen in profile, a site open to the sun but sheltered from the wind: and, my dear Kathy, a place as yet undiscovered by anybody but me.'

'Brilliant,' exclaimed Kathy, echoing the latest in-word from Highminster. 'Absolutely brilliant! Off with the rucksacks and on with Mrs Gibbs' "special for today".'

Special it certainly was: crustless sandwiches delicately cut as if to grace the tea table of a Victorian deanery; fillings of home-made salmon mousse, of beef and egg and lettuce; Stilton spread on biscuits and peaches already peeled!

'And we honour the feast,' said Martin, 'with a light wine from Italy,' extracting with a conjuror's flourish a bottle of Verdicchio from a refrigerated holder. 'In so doing, we lighten our load for the return journey.'

They rounded off Mrs Gibbs' 'special' with black coffee and settled for a brief siesta – a time for meditation as Martin put it.

'And will your meditation be disturbed by a little sunbathing?'

'My dear girl, you can do anything you like up here provided you don't leave litter lying about.'

Martin lay back and his eyes closed.

Kathy eyed the man beside her, his breathing regular, his body still. She wriggled out of her slacks, unbuttoned her shirt and shuffled off her shoes. She looked again at her companion and was dimly aware that somebody outside herself – a Lakeland sprite or joking Puck or pagan Pan – was urging her forward. Suddenly Martin seemed to her immensely desirable. Somebody – surely it could not be Mrs Joseph Selby of Melbridge – was making sleep impossible. Was this, she wondered, how Eve had felt in the Garden of Eden? Did the Spirit of Midsummer's Day continue to overrule reason in this beautiful land? She felt in a crazy daredevil mood. She

115

remembered the word 'pixolated' from that priceless film *Mr Deeds Comes to Town*. She smiled happily at the memory. Yes, this was it – she was 'pixolated' and very wide awake.

She edged a little closer to Martin. Was he really asleep? She kissed him lightly on the forehead and in a low-pitched voice she hardly recognised whispered into his ear, 'Martin, I want to make love to you.'

There was a slight stirring. 'Kathy, what's that you're saying?'

'Nothing,' she said, but she turned towards him until her thigh was resting against his. The strange voice made a slight change in its appeal: 'Martin, I want you to make love to me.'

She waited. His left hand stole across and touched her cheek. Her fingers took his and drew them lower. The voice spoke again, 'Why should we not make love together?'

Without a word, he turned and gently pushed her on to her back. He bent over her, looked into her eyes and saw daring and expectation. In his eyes she saw questions formed and questions answering themselves. Her hands guided him. He kissed her as she had wanted him to do these last few days ... they were locked together, silent until that moment of ecstacy when each gave everything to the other ... together, they shared the joy of lovers ... up there, away from civilisation's traffic, they felt themselves to be part of Creation itself, sharing in a mystery of Nature's world beyond the range of human reason.

Minutes passed ... or was it hours? ... and they were still lying side by side on the hidden ground that only Martin knew. They were like swimmers who, ignoring the warning signals, are carried away by currents they cannot withstand until, by the grace of God or the turn of the tide, they are hurled back by the waves on to a patch of dry land which they find hard to recognise.

But the character of their relationship had changed. Their conversation was no longer concerned with a probing of times past. The abstractions of history had given place to more intimate talk. It was as if confessing to each other the restraints and problems of their own lives was a refuge from discussing the consequence of what they each in their innermost hearts knew must be an afternoon snatched out of time, but not to be savoured any the less for that.

On that magic hillside above Langdale the sun gradually lost its warmth. It was high time to pack up and return to civilisation. Kathy kissed Martin once more before shouldering her rucksack and following him back to the car.

The telephone was ringing as they entered the house. Joseph Selby speaking and was his wife available? A moment later, Kathy was listening as Joe reported his activities, item by item, in his own precise way.

Richard Fagg? Joe had guided the wretched man through his police interview – he was going to supply valuable evidence when the case came to court – might reasonably expect a suspended sentence.

'Lord Melchester? Delighted with formation of Melbridge Golf Club Ltd. Expect to be invited to dine at the Court. Oh yes, you too Kathy. New dress I'd say: what do you think?

'Becky? Looking after me splendidly – I took her to dine at the Feathers last night.'

'What's that, Joe?'

'More when we meet, darling. It was Eleanor Grant's idea, really.

'Final item. *The Times* reports that Roger Powell is leaving Highminster next year to take up an appointment as headmaster of a co-ed school in Sussex. Must stop now. Remember me to all. Will meet the London train at Melchester tomorrow. Longing to see you . . . Goodnight, my dear.'

And the line went dead.

Kathy replaced the receiver. She felt she was blushing, she knew she did not wish to see or talk to anybody until she had, so to speak, recovered her balance. The intrusion of Joe's call into her Lakeland world, though fully expected, had come at the wrong moment. She would go to her bedroom, get out of her holiday shirt and slacks, enjoy a bath and put on the clothes she would wear for the return journey to Melbridge.

At dinner, on that final night of the holiday, nobody remarked on her change of dress. The boys may not have noticed: they were so busy showing their photos. If Martin noticed, he made no comment, for which Kathy was grateful. If there was any constraint in adult conversation, it went unnoticed as the boys reported on the activities

117

of their new friend, William Bailey who, at Danny's request, had remembered some of the Cumbrian folk songs which in his early days had enlivened traditional festivities at Midsummer and Harvest.

'Brilliant tunes,' Danny confirmed, 'good for dancing as well as singing. I've transcribed two of them, note by note, on Mr Bailey's piano. I'll fill in the harmonies, add a few fal-lals and play them back to him when we next meet. Which reminds me, Mum, talking of meeting people, Major Wrattenley has agreed to drive us into Preston early enough for us to meet Rosie Harbottle for elevenses.'

'It was Danny's idea really,' Martin added, 'but it struck me, Kathy, that you too might like to have a word with the lady. And you'll have lots of time as the Royal Scot only leaves Preston at twelve thirty.'

'Just right for lunch on the train,' the boys added together, 'and we are advised by Mr Bailey to choose fish when travelling to London but stick to meat on the return journey north.'

Much later Kathy sat in front of the dressing table in her nightie and stared at herself in the mirror. Her mind was going round in small circles. Joe – Martin, Melbridge – Rydal, Danny, Becky – Mrs Grant, Fagg – Melchester, Danny – Peter, Danny – Rosie, Danny . . .

The repetition of Danny's name told her what to do. She reached for a wrap, went to the boys' room, found them both in bed reading and kissed each head protruding from the bedclothes. 'Sleep well, both of you. Perhaps Ratty will join us next holidays in Melbridge. Goodnight, goodnight.'

She shut the boys' door gently, as she had always done at home, and after a moment's hesitation, returned to her own room.

17

Kathy was a very worried woman.

Eight days after returning home, she was still spending most of the day and part of the night engaged in futile argument with herself.

Her reaction to Joe's phone call to Rydal had been, she knew, totally unreasonable. The poor man had done no more than he had promised to do – telling her what was happening in Melbridge and confirming the arrangements for meeting her train.

This feeling of irritation had boiled up again at Preston station after Martin had left her and Rosie to finalise the arrangements for Danny's school term. But really, as Rosie made clear, there was nothing to discuss.

'Your husband, Mrs Selby, has been ever so helpful. He's sent us a typed letter on his office paper setting out our lodging terms, which Bert considers most generous, and he's sent a cheque to cover the first term.'

Rosie had paused for a moment to take a bite of the Eccles cake which Danny had ordered. But almost at once she was back with more news of Joe's activities.

'Had a phone call from a very nice gentleman who knows your father, Danny; a lawyer with an address in Winckley Square. He hopes to meet you once you're settled in, and he has mentioned your name to the vicar of St John the Baptist. Mind you, me and Bert are Methodists . . .' As Rosie rambled on Kathy tried to listen politely. But she was inwardly raging. Why hadn't Joe told her what he was doing? For that matter, she thought resentfully, he could have taken her and Danny with him when he went to see the man in Winckley Square in the first place, instead of sending them out sightseeing, and treating her no better than an office junior at Selby & Leadbitter.

By the time they boarded the Royal Scot she had developed a headache and settled for black coffee and biscuits which in no way put Danny off enjoying his three-course lunch with salmon 'straight from the Highlands, sir'. With the insight which so many boys of his age possess, he did not bother her with small talk, but looked after the tickets and her suitcase, finding the taxi at Euston and the right platform at Waterloo. But she was not to be comforted.

At Melchester station an excited Becky had raced down the platform to greet her.

'Guess what, Mum! This morning, passed my driving test, first go!'

Behind Becky was Joe, clearly delighted with a daughter who bore such a marked resemblance to the young bride he'd married nearly twenty years earlier. And Kathy hardly knew how to reciprocate their welcome. In the heady Lakeland air, she had forgotten the date of Becky's driving test!

Now, eight days passing still brought no relief. Joe provided her with morning tea before leaving for the office at the usual time. Danny was off on his bike to Abbotshaven to talk with the Professor about Mr Bailey's Cumbrian folk tunes; and Becky seemed happy to potter in the kitchen without much maternal intervention.

It was while she was lunching with Becky that Kathy learnt of the dinner party at the Feathers.

'It was all about Dad's golf club project,' Becky explained. 'How much do you know, Mum?'

'Only that a company has been formed, planning permission obtained and a golf course architect's draft plans submitted.'

'Well, I can tell you, Mum, it's got much further than that. It's difficult to know where to start.'

'Why not start with the dinner party?'

That, after all, was the part that intrigued Kathy: and her interest grew as Becky told the tale of her evening out.

'Right then, we'll start with the dinner. "Her Ladyship" (that's what Dad calls Mrs Grant in private, you know) – she was hosting the party in her private suite which looks out on to Dad's old office in Feathers Lane. The four of us – that's me, Dad, Mrs Grant and her brother-in-law, Julian Grant, are all dressed for the occasion – Dad looks absolutely smashing in his new dinner jacket – it's a real "posh" affair, you see, which I understand Her Ladyship likes to arrange from time to time, generally with some new idea in her mind. Anyhow, the menu, Mum, was exactly right, personally served by her chef Alphonse ... duck pâté, Dover sole, already boned, with *pommes dauphinoise* and little herby tomatoes followed by fresh fruit salad ... Oh, yes, and a white wine called Pouilly something or other which Mr Grant was very pleased with.'

Kathy interrupted. 'It sounds terrific, darling, but who is this Julian Grant? And why was he invited?'

'Because of this new golf club of course. Mr Grant's up to his eyes in it; he's been brought into the planning by Dad and Bob Withers.'

'But why get him involved?'

'Simple, Mum, simple. First because he's managing director of the Melchester Breweries and is putting money into the enterprise in return for the franchise on catering and bar. Secondly, because he's a keen single-figure golfer. So he knows what the golfers actually want. He's very impressed by the course architect's plans. Told me it would be like Rye: two nine-hole loops extending east and west of the club house. As I looked at bit dim, he drew a picture for me – like a figure of eight with the club house at the crossing point.'

'So where's this club house going to be, Becky?'

'Ah, that's where Lord Melchester and Bob Withers come into the picture. They've agreed not to renew the tenancy of Saxby's farm. The land not required for the golf course will now come under Bob Withers' Home Farm control, while the farmhouse and outbuildings will become the club house and professional shop.'

Kathy was amazed at the speed with which the golf club project was going forward, and no less at her daughter's mastery of and interest in the detail of it all. Treating her like an adult had made her think like one. Kathy had a momentary pang for a childhood ended. But at the same time she was proud for her pretty and uncomplicated daughter.

'Well, thank you, love, for bringing me up to date. I'm longing to hear more, but I really must get across to East Street to find something suitable to wear at this Melchester Court party your father's been talking about. But one final question: how did you come to be included in Her Ladyship's invitation?'

'It must have been because you were still up north. But in your absence Mr Joseph Selby's daughter was officially present to voice the opinion of Melbridge women!'

'Come off it, Becky, you're joking!'

'No, honestly, Mum, it's true. You know most golf clubs must be really prehistoric. But Eleanor Grant and Dad have persuaded their partners to give men and women equal members' rights at this new club – shock, horror! No, really, it's a brilliant idea – I told them so – and Dad looked so pleased. Between you and me, Mum, I think it was really his idea but he cunningly gave Mrs Grant credit for it. He's very clever at persuading people, isn't he?'

Clever at persuading people, or clever at saying nothing? – Kathy's thoughts were a mixture of anger and mortification as she crossed the Close. She was horribly aware that she'd taken no interest in Joe's golf course plans nor, for that matter, in the problems of Richard Fagg.

She looked in at La Belle Femme in East Street and then at Collington's – but in her present mood, she didn't know what she wanted so of course she didn't find it and returned from the shops totally frustrated. She could only think of this barrier which had grown up between herself and Joe precipitating her into her moment of midsummer madness in Langdale.

She was still arguing with herself, as she crossed the Close. She must have been walking at less than her normal brisk pace, for she was overtaken by Ted Baynes striding from the vicarage to take the mid-week Evensong in the parish church. He fell into step beside her.

'Hello, Kathy. Something on your mind?'

Was her desperation so obvious, then? But she clutched the rescuing hand. She knew what she had to do.

'Ted, I need your help,' she faltered on. 'No, it's not about Danny, or Becky or Joe – just something I have to tell you.'

'Of course, Kathy. No hurry to get home? Then why don't you join me after the service? It's only a short affair, you know, which we take in the Lady Chapel. No music, though if Harry Leng comes in, he generally plays a voluntary before the service starts. Only a few people present, mostly for their own private reasons – some wanting to express thanks or to pray for family or friends, others attracted on their way home by the lights in the church. At this time of year, with the daylight fading, the ancient stone seems to speak to people . . . it's a very personal sort of service, you know . . . just hang around after it's over, Kathy, I'll wait for you by the north door.' Ted Baynes hurried ahead.

As if under some inner compulsion, Kathy followed him into the ancient church and took her place in the Lady Chapel. The organ was playing, the soft notes rising to the high rafters. Beyond the chapel, the chancel and nave were suffused in a dim mysterious light. As the notes of the organ died away Ted Baynes, unrobed, crossed the church from the vestry by the north door and took his place at the small prayer desk.

Breaking into the silence came the lovely cadence of seventeenth-century English, most gently spoken:

> Almighty and most merciful Father,
> We have erred and strayed
> from Thy ways like lost sheep . . .

18

The short service ended, Kathy continued to sit in the Lady Chapel while the other worshippers dispersed. She guessed there had been about twenty people present: among them, a lad keeping a date with his girl, an old lady who had polished the altar-plate of St Peter and St Paul for as long as Kathy could remember, a well-dressed young man probably from one of the Southside offices, two women with heavy shopping bags, and the easily recognised district nurse. An incongruous lot, indeed. What, Kathy wondered, had attracted them to the church on this weekday afternoon – gratitude, anxiety, loneliness? Or was each of them seeking some indefinable quality called 'peace of mind'?

She rose, in her turn, to walk across the church to the vestry by the north door. Involuntarily she began to repeat to herself the familiar words of the Evensong Collects which she had just heard: 'Lighten our darkness we beseech Thee, O Lord . . . Give unto Thy servants that peace which the world cannot give . . .'

For a moment she hesitated, looking east into the darkness of the choir and chancel, and then west down the majestic nave, mysteriously lit by the rays of the setting sun filtering through the side windows of the south transept.

Then she caught sight of Edward Baynes, his friendly figure silhouetted against the light of the vestry door.

'Come in, Kathy,' he said. 'Come in and tell me what's troubling you.'

He preceded her up a flight of stone steps leading from the vestry to a small room above the north door of the church. It was warm and carpeted, and furnished with a table, a bookcase and four straight-backed chairs, but otherwise devoid of any decoration except for a small cross hanging on the wall facing Kathy.

'My private place of refuge,' Edward explained, 'and except for the cross which once belonged to my mother, furnished entirely by your father-in-law, my dear old chess-playing friend. I well remember the nice things he used to say about you.'

'Yes, he was a wonderful man. The children and I loved the way he used to drop in for tea. But he wouldn't say nice things about me if he knew what I have to tell you.'

Kathy's voice dropped. 'But I have to tell somebody ... you see, Edward,' the simple words suddenly burst from her like water from a breached dam, 'you see, Edward, I've been unfaithful to Joe.'

The vicar heard the distress in her voice, saw her fingers digging into the palms of her hands. He reacted very quickly.

'And this happened on your Lake District holiday after Joe was called back to do what he could for the unhappy Richard Fagg? Is that right?'

'Yes. But I have to say that it might have happened anywhere ... anyhow ... any time. And, more than that, I took joy in what I did. I was excited ... felt young again ... I don't know how to put it ...' Kathy stumbled on. 'You see, for some time I'd been feeling neglected, cut out of Joe's thinking ... He seemed totally obsessed with his business activities: they were all top secret. He shared the children with me, but nothing else. I'd become no more than a housekeeper. He didn't understand a woman's need for physical love.'

'But something turned your thoughts into action?'

'Yes, the something was Danny's unhappiness at Highminster. We travelled north, as I think you know, to settle the problem of his education: and I planned to use our break in the north to give Joe and me a real holiday together. And then – no sooner had we settled the school problem – Joe had to rush back to advise this wretched drug-pusher.'

'And that's when the string broke?'

'Yes, I suppose so.' Kathy was sobbing now and fiddling in her handbag for a handkerchief, as she filled in the circumstances of her one compulsive moment. 'But you mustn't blame Martin.

126

He only did what I wanted him to do.'

'Enough, my dear, enough.' There was nothing of judgement in Edward Baynes' voice. 'Passions and emotions are rarely governed by logic. We'll concentrate on the simple fact that you've broken the Seventh Commandment. Or – put it another way – you've fallen down on the promise you made before God and your friends when you married Joe, nearly twenty years ago, in St Wilfred's. And now you come to me to say you're sorry for what you've done. Is that right?'

Kathy's eyes looked straight at the priest. No outside sound penetrated the small room.

'Yes,' she said. 'I am very sorry. Every day since I came back to Melbridge, I've been ashamed of the love I enjoyed above Langdale. Yes, I'm very sorry.'

The priest turned to the bookshelf beside him, pulled out a prayer book and opened it at the Collect for Ash Wednesday before handing it to Kathy.

'Now, my dear, let me speak in my capacity as a man of God, ordained to be your vicar: and let me make two points, both of them for your comfort. First, the Bible teaches that, in God's eyes, all of us have sinned: yes, Kathy, your parents and Joe – as well as you and I. We all stand before God in need of forgiveness. And secondly, Jesus has revealed to us that the God we worship is a God of Love who forgives those who truly repent. Therefore,' Edward paused and spoke very slowly, 'because you have repented God will grant you forgiveness and pardon and freedom from any sense of guilt.'

The priest crossed the room and placed his hands on Kathy's bowed head. 'Bless you, my child,' he said. 'Go forth from this place in peace. May God have mercy on you.'

He resumed his seat and opened his prayer book. 'Before we go our separate ways,' he said, 'I'd like to read one of Cranmer's loveliest prayers. Read it with me, if you like: or look at it again when you get home.'

In the silence of the small room Edward Baynes prayed. 'Almighty and everlasting God who hatest nothing that thou has made, and dost forgive the sins of all them that are penitent, create and make in us true and contrite hearts, that we worthily lamenting our sins and acknowledging our wretchedness, may obtain of thee, the God of all mercy, perfect remission and forgiveness, through Jesus Christ our Lord. Amen.'

Edward closed his prayer book deliberately, saying nothing which might detract from the words of the prayer.

Then, he led Kathy down the narrow flight of stone steps. Only as they left the church and emerged into the Close did he speak again.

'One last thought, my dear: I have to warn you that a contrite heart does not absolve you from taking certain positive actions.'

'You mean?'

'Simply that you still have to choose between Joe and Martin Wrattenley.'

'Oh, but I must stay with Joe and Becky and Daniel, that's for sure. I couldn't leave them, could I?'

'Thank God for that, Kathy. But it follows that you have to tell Joe what you've told me. That won't be easy, will it? For you or for Joe?'

'I must do this, must I?'

'I think so, Kathy. You can't live a lie for ever: and the sooner you tell Joe, the better. No fine words, mind you – no prepared speeches ... just be honest with him as you've been with me. The man we both know is good and kind, and surely quick to forgive. Come to think of it, the way he's been working flat out to save a man whose criminal connections have caused such trouble to his practice is not a bad example of compassion and forgiveness, and a far cry from Grandma Selby's visions of judgement and hellfire for the sinner! So courage, Kathy, and honesty. You and Joe will both be in my prayers.'

Their ways parted – Kathy moving across the Close towards the old grammar school and Ockenham Drive, Edward Baynes setting off towards the vicarage on Selby's Pavement. But some further thought must have crossed his mind, for he suddenly turned and called across to Kathy, an encouraging smile on his face.

'A parting thought, my dear. You may have to put up with a lot of talk from Joe about this new golf project. I think you could do worse than give golf a go. My wife and I enjoy our holiday golf, and she was delighted when I retired from the cricket scene. Just a parting thought – something to occupy your mind on the way home.'

Kathy reached Ockenham Drive without meeting anybody. Her mind was a mixture of apprehension and courage, but she seemed to walk with a lighter step. Unwittingly, her feet marched to a rhythmic beat: 'Penitence, forgiveness, guilt-free, golf', which she recited to herself as far as the gate by the grammar school, where she stopped and laughed aloud at the ridiculous sequence.

Opening the front door of number ten she picked up a note left in the hall by Becky, kept in place by a paperweight given to Kathy many years ago by Grandpa Selby.

The note in Becky's bold handwriting was brief and to the point.

'Have taken car to collect Sue and Linda and on to Melchester for party given by Ma Thesinger. Chicken casserole cooked. Heat up 25 minutes Gas 6. Also fresh fruit salad in fridge. Be back before midnight. Don't wait up. Becky.'

Dear Becky, so competent and precise, just like Joe. And Danny? She knew that he was spending the day at Chopin House in Abbotshaven, rehearsing under the Professor for some charity concert. Harry Leng had promised to bring him home.

So she would be alone with Joe this very evening. It had to be the moment of truth. Remember, Edward had said, no fine words, no prepared speeches, just be honest . . .

She found she was still holding in her hand the little paperweight, an eccentrically shaped piece of Cornish granite mounted on a wooden base. It was something Grandpa Selby had put together as a schoolboy, and he'd given it to her, almost apologetically, on one of his teatime visits to Ockenham Drive. But now his words came back to her with a rush of clarity. 'A small reminder, my dear, from the days of my youth, but something which actually won my father's commendation. His speech, as you know, was constantly laced with biblical quotations. On this occasion he added that it put him in mind of the words of Zechariah: "You must never despise the day of small things."'

That was really Grandpa Selby's guiding principle in life. He was more interested in the problems of the small town and the small homes around him than he was in national issues and world politics with which the papers were filled.

Kathy looked again at the little paperweight in her hands. People said that it was Isaac Selby who had persuaded Edward Baynes to stay on as Vicar of Melbridge rather than seek higher appointment. Perhaps Edward had also been infected by his friend's philosophy.

Kathy was still standing in the hall holding Isaac Selby's schoolboy creation when she saw her husband approaching the house. She opened the door.

'Had a good day, Joe? Becky and Danny are out for the evening, so we have the place to ourselves. It's dinner for two tonight.'

19

Kathy sat, still and silent, on one end of the sofa in the living-room. She was listening intently to Joe's movements as he followed his regular return-from-the-office habits. She couldn't be sure, but it sounded as if his steps were slower than usual.

After the peck of a kiss at the front door, he had disappeared upstairs as he always did. There, he would loosen his tie and take off his jacket, draping it on a coathanger that he kept for this specific purpose. Next, he would exchange his walking shoes for some old house-slippers which he loved as other men love antiques ('they'll last my time, Kathy'). Then he would proceed to wash his hands, as if he was cleaning up after a day in a city stinking of smoke and petrol fumes though it would be hard to find any place of work cleaner than Selby's Pavement in Melbridge. Finally he would don a bottle-green cardigan – a Christmas present she'd knitted for him some five years earlier. Apart from its sentimental value, it provided him with two pockets, one containing a clean handkerchief, the other a ballpoint. Thus equipped, he would return to his armchair in the living-room where, as like as not, he would take a further look at the *Financial Times*, occasionally making notes on a small pad he kept beside him.

It was only after placing Becky's chicken casserole in the preheated oven that Kathy had returned to her place on the sofa. All this time she kept repeating certain words to herself in a sort of exercise in auto-suggestion – 'simplicity', 'honesty', 'no speeches' – which somewhat absurdly kept time with Joe's footsteps as she heard him descending the stairs.

She smiled as he appeared at the door, open shirted and wearing the old slippers and her knitted cardigan, exactly as she had envisaged. But this evening he did not cross the room to his familiar chair. Instead, he came and sat beside her, put an arm around her shoulder, and his grey eyes gazed into hers.

There was a trembling urgency in his voice. 'Tell me, darling,' he said, coming straight to the point. 'Tell me what's come between us. What's the trouble?'

Joe's voice brought Kathy that sense of relief an actor feels as he comes on stage on an opening night. Rehearsals were over. The moment of truth had arrived.

Very simply she told Joe the story of her Lakeland madness – first her fury at his sudden return to Melbridge in order to champion the cause of the wretched Richard Fagg, then the compensating joy of the Grasmere walk, the warmth of her reception in the house beside Rydal Water, her physical desire for a man and her delight in Martin's easy companionship until finally she reached her deliberate provocation of the man and the subsequent lovemaking in the secret place above Langdale.

She hid nothing, her words soft, almost whispered, her eyes lowered. While she was speaking, Joe remained silent, but Kathy could feel his hand tightening its grip on her arm and sense his grey eyes fixed on her. Then, as her words faded away, the hand relaxed its grip and seemed to push her away as if to make space between them.

'So I was right,' he said, his normally musical voice unnaturally harsh. 'It's happened exactly as I feared and I must accept the blame.'

'What are you saying, Joe? What do you mean?' Kathy could not hold back her tears. 'I'm trying to say I'm sorry for what I've done, when you turn on yourself as if it were all your fault.'

'But Kathy, my darling, don't you see?' Joe drew her close to him, kissing her eyes and running his fingers through her hair. 'I wasn't blind. I saw your frustration on that first evening at Rydal – and still I went away, without a word of regret, to advise and represent young Fagg at his police interrogation. The moment I was back in Melbridge, I realised what a fool I'd been – all the priorities wrong, giving a drug-pusher's crimes precedence over your happiness – and then, when I phoned a few days later, I experienced a terrible sense of alienation, as if I was an unwanted intruder. It was my fault, Kathy, not yours.'

He pulled the clean handkerchief out of his cardigan pocket and wiped her eyes. 'So where do we go from here? Do you want to go back to Martin and share his life?'

'Leave you, Joe? No, no: not if you can forgive me.' She smiled at him as she took the handkerchief from him and returned it to his cardigan pocket. 'I'll tell you where we go from here. Straight into the kitchen to enjoy Becky's chicken casserole.'

Joe only posed one question as they emerged from the living-room. Did anybody except Martin know of the affair? And he seemed relieved when Kathy told him of her meeting with Ted Baynes.

'Bless you,' he said. 'That means I can talk with him, too.'

There were no more personal confessions or recriminations that night. What was past was past. For the moment at least, the subject was closed. Kathy's confession and Joe's unexpected response to it had defused the tension between husband and wife. You would have detected no constraints, no abrupt sentences left unfinished, nor awkward silences, as Joe and Kathy enjoyed Becky's kitchen meal.

Kathy had the intuition to perceive that her husband, normally so tight-lipped about his business activities, was longing to tell her what he'd been doing while she and Danny had been away. And now, in answer to her prompting, he told her how, on his advice, Richard Fagg had disclosed to the police everything he knew about the paymasters from whom he had been taking his orders.

It was a truly pathetic story. Evidently the young man had been spotted in a betting shop, quickly identified as a compulsive gambler, traced to a solicitor's office in Lincoln's Inn and, in due course, offered an after-hours job which required some rudimentary knowledge of Company Law.

Private companies were to be formed, each one linked with the acquisition and sale of residential property. Surplus funds were deposited in local building societies and, from time to time, withdrawn for the purchase of luxury houses.

In these activities, Fagg's legal knowledge and qualifications were invaluable. The anonymous bosses were more than satisfied. Payments were generous and regular, sufficient at least to get Richard Fagg clear of his debts. Whatever his suspicions, it was only after he was deeply involved that he guessed the horrible source of the funds he was handling and the nature of the nameless criminals he was serving.

Joe paused for a moment's speculation. Then he said, 'It was, I like to think, an honest attempt by Richard to get clear of his paymaster that caused him to apply for the job at Selby and Leadbitter.'

'And the bosses wouldn't let him off the hook?'

'That's right, Kathy. Their suspicions were aroused and they kept him under observation. But two incidents upset their plans. First, Eleanor Grant took exception to the people consorting with him at the Feathers. And secondly – and quite separately – the Customs men uncovered the illicit cargo being offloaded by these get-rich-quick yachtsmen at Abbotshaven.'

'So where's Richard Fagg now?'

'Well away from Melbridge, I'm glad to say: somewhere in the Midlands, holding a temporary job with an estate agent and reporting regularly to the local police. Of course, they will expect him to supply them with a lot of corroborative evidence, but with a bit of luck he should escape with a suspended sentence.'

'You feel sorry for him, don't you?'

'Yes, I suppose I do, though I've also felt the lawyer's traditional duty to do what he can for his client.'

A half-smile lit up Joe's face as he continued.

'There's something very sad, you know, about a compulsive gambler. Like an alcoholic, he finds it terribly difficult to kick the habit. And if you want to go gambling every week you either need a magic system or funds on the scale of Lord Melchester's.'

Joe and Kathy were back in the living-room enjoying instant coffee when Kathy reverted to the case of Lord Melchester.

'Tell me, Joe, has His Lordship a part to play in this golf project Becky's been talking about? It seems to have got a lot further than those figures you were adding up on the journey to Preston.'

'Further? I should say so. Further indeed than Becky knows. This man, Julian Grant, has supplied us with the overdrive the project needed.' And Kathy was glad to hear the note of enthusiasm back in Joe's voice, perhaps an echo of Grandpa Selby's voice, dating back to the days when he had persuaded his fellow citizens to establish the pedestrian walkway now known as Selby's Pavement.

Joe sketched in the salient points with the economy of words which had always been a characteristic of his court appearance.

'And there are really going to be enough people prepared to pay £10,000 for life membership?'

'Yes,' Joe confirmed, 'there are three of Julian's friends in Melchester that I know of for a start, and two people in Melbridge – Tom Gutteridge and young Collington. But there will also be family and school membership plans, all based on an annual subscription of £250.' He looked at his wife. 'What do you think, Kathy?'

'It's great, Joe. Why not give it a go? But who is going to teach us?'

'No problem,' he said. Julian had secured the services of a Glasgow professional, Sandy MacNaughton, who in January would be taking up residence in the old farmhouse, complete with Mrs MacNaughton and two small children.

'Steady, Joe. Aren't you going too fast? There won't be a course to play on!'

But Joe was ready with an answer. There would be a practice ground using the existing grassland beside the old farmhouse immediately available. 'Bob's mowers are out already and Sandy will start his golf school as soon as his family has settled in. I thought I might be the first to apply for a lesson.'

'Fair enough, Joe. And tell Mr MacNaughton to register me as his first woman pupil.'

They were still talking and laughing over details about women's rights and family membership when Harry Leng dropped off Danny.

There could be no more talk about the Melbridge Golf Club. Kathy produced Digestive biscuits and a cup of hot chocolate for their son while he told them how the Professor had recruited him for another charity concert to be held at Abbotshaven.

'In aid of the Polish Red Cross,' he said. 'But the point is, Dad, the Professor has assigned me the violin part in Beethoven's Archduke Trio. You'll buy some tickets, won't you? It will be my last Saturday before I travel north to Preston.'

What a day to remember. Moving so swiftly from misery to happiness. Becky would let herself in when she returned from her school reunion. Meanwhile it was bed for the rest of the family and sleep undisturbed.

The last thing Kathy remembered was a few words from the prayer that Edward Baynes had read: 'A contrite heart, O Lord, thou wilt not despise.'

20

For Kathy one unavoidable duty remained – writing a letter to Martin Wrattenley.

Next morning, as soon as Joe had left for the office, she sat down at the small desk beside the front window of the living-room, determined not to be distracted from the task by the demands of her children or the sight of neighbours passing by.

She started briskly enough with an envelope stamped and addressed to Major Wrattenley, RE, MC. There followed, rather more slowly, a stilted letter of thanks, about as colourless as those duty letters she'd been ordered to write in her childhood days. Her bold handwriting managed to take her over the page. For a moment, she hesitated about the ending before settling for 'yours affectionately and gratefully, Kathy'.

She was on the point of sealing the envelope when something inside her took over. She snatched another sheet of writing paper from the desk drawer, headed it 'postscript' and her ballpoint raced forward at a speed beyond her control.

I have now settled back into the routine of Melbridge life with Joe and our two children which means I may never again accompany you to your heavenly, secret place on the hillside above Langdale. But I want you to know, you dear, understanding man, that I shall always treasure the magic hours we shared on that sun-kissed hill. In my heart they will never be forgotten.

For Martin from Kathy, with love.

That was that. Kathy folded the second sheet of paper very carefully, and hurried, almost ran with the sealed envelope to the post box at the corner of Ockenham Drive.

She was back, thank God, on the solid ground of Melbridge life. Heading down the Melchester Road she turned left at the grammar school and thence across the Close to East Street to keep a date with her mother at Dolly Hayward's.

Liz Hardingham was already seated at a table for two. 'There you are, my darling. Come and sit down and tell me about your stay in Lakeland. Me, I've settled for a large cup of Costa Rica coffee and a slice of Dolly's chocolate cake. I know it's bad for the figure, but that's my problem – not yours.'

Mother and daughter had so much to talk about. Kathy needed to explain how she and Joe had finally decided to let Danny finish his schooling in Preston.

'I'm afraid it's a big disappointment for both of us. But we've all come to recognise that Danny's an odd number. He'll always want to go his own way. Anyway, for better or for worse, he's off to Lancashire next term.'

The coffee and cakes arrived and the older woman took over the running, with a round-up of the rest of the Hardingham family news and views, the latter mostly prefaced with 'Jack thinks' or 'in Jack's view'. But Kathy was not fooled – her father generally accepted his wife's lead.

Kathy's young brother Jimmy had come through Cirencester Agricultural College with an even greater enthusiasm for a farmer's life. 'No sign of leaving home – and Jack is so pleased. Meanwhile, he's helping Bob Withers at the Home Farm and that part of Saxby's which hasn't been sold to this new golf club venture ... which reminds me, Kathy! What do you know of Eleanor Grant's brother-in-law, Julian?'

Kathy laughed. 'Not much more, I suspect, than you do from the information Becky must have given you after her upmarket dinner party at the Feathers. But I know that Joe and Bob Withers think the world of him. I gather he's got the project into the fast lane, with Melchester Breweries putting a lot of money into it. Do you know more than I do?'

'Not really, dear, though Jack speaks well of him. But Jimmy seems to have taken a fancy to his daughter and she's already persuaded him to become a member of this new golf club. He's hoping, I think, to persuade Jack to take up one of the family memberships they're planning. Comes of him seeing a lot of Bob Withers, and getting an inside view of life at Melchester Court.'

'No trouble there, I hope?' Kathy knew how much Joe and Bob were relying on Freddy Melchester to support the golf venture.

'No trouble as far as the golf is concerned, my dear ... but if Jimmy's to be believed, there's no golden future for the Melchester marriage ... Lady Melchester has no friends up at the Court ... Poor Freddy ... Not perhaps the strongest of men, but at heart, a kind person that everybody wants to help.'

'Well, I'm very glad to receive a little inside information. You know Joe and I are supposed to be dining with them next month? Actually, my immediate concern is to find something suitable to wear. Any ideas, Mother? I couldn't find anything remotely possible at La Belle Femme or Collington's.'

On her mother's advice, Kathy tried a new shop, which had recently opened and was happy to find exactly what she wanted, a dress in green and primrose colours which complemented her auburn hair and brown eyes – a dress which she knew would please Joe and even catch the eye of the underrated, henpecked Freddy Melchester.

On reaching home, she made herself a chicken and lettuce sandwich and took it out to the garden together with one of those Mary Stewart Merlin novels she was currently enjoying. Nothing to disturb her ... Becky out with friends ... Danny and his violin away with the Professor at Chopin House. Both children would be off her hands very soon now. Danny to Preston and Becky to Canterbury. Almost automatically, she checked the dates in her diary. Suddenly, she was gripped by a new anxiety. She had missed out on her monthly period. She checked back ... not a doubt about it. Still, you never know. She'd had a lot of anxiety ...

It was only after another three weeks had hurried by, with Danny safely lodged with the Harbottles in Preston and Becky with her Morris gone to Canterbury for her first term at university that Kathy summoned up courage to resolve her doubts. With a sinking feeling, she phoned Oliver Carstairs for an appointment.

21

There was no longer room for doubt. On Kathy's second visit to the surgery on Southside Oliver Carstairs confirmed that the urine pregnancy test was positive, and reckoned a baby could be expected in the following April.

The doctor had been slightly worried by Kathy's ill-concealed anxiety when she had first consulted him. He knew her forthright character far too well to be deceived. Now he was sure Mrs Joseph Selby's pregnancy was unexpected . . . unwanted . . . almost certainly a neglect of the usual precautions. As he watched her hands clutching her handbag and listened to her effort to control her voice, he knew his diagnosis was anything but welcome.

'No doubt.' He spoke as gently as he could in answer to her reiterated question, and moved from his desk to sit beside her. He was very fond of her and wondered how best to be reassuring.

'You mustn't worry, Kathy. There's no reason why a new baby shouldn't bring as much joy to you and Joe as Becky and Danny have done. I know Danny's rising sixteen, but you'll be surprised how quickly the gap in years narrows down. As a matter of fact, I myself am a post-war child born into a pre-war family and, if my experience is anything to go by, your new baby will receive all the love in the world from the older children.

'Mind you, I realise this will cause a bit of disruption in the home . . . even a delay in the start of the tennis season.'

Receiving no answering smile he hurried on.

'Promise me not to worry. Go and tell Joe, and let him do the worrying.'

Oliver helped her from her chair and escorted her to the door.

'Goodbye for the moment. I'll arrange to see you in a month's time.'

He lingered for a time at his fine front door, watching Kathy's trim figure crossing the Close.

'I wonder,' he said to himself. 'I wonder what on earth has happened. Kathy Selby isn't the sort of woman to make mistakes like this.'

Desperate thoughts were hammering away in Kathy's mind. What should she do? Go to London and have an abortion? She looked up at the oaks and elms for guidance but the falling leaves of autumn had no advice to offer. Should she leave Melbridge before her pregnancy showed; give birth in some out-of-the-way anonymous clinic and get the baby adopted? The empty seats in the Close and the lichened gravestones stayed silent and unfeeling. Or were they telling her to stay in this small town and face the gossip when it came? She could ride that sort of storm easily enough. But apart from Joe, there were still people who had to be informed: her parents for instance ... Becky and Danny ... Edward Baynes ... and where and when did Martin come into the picture? She began talking to herself as she had so often done while facing tough opposition on the tennis court. 'Keep calm, Kathy Selby, get a grip and, for Heaven's sake, fight to win.'

When she let herself into number ten the place felt horribly empty. She wandered round the house disconsolate. No music came from the record player in Danny's room. Becky's room, unnaturally tidy, was devoid of personality except for a much-loved teddybear peeping from the bedcover. Kathy returned to the living-room and slumped on to the sofa where she had first told Joe of her Lakeland love affair.

Joe – she remembered Oliver Carstairs' words: 'Tell Joe and let him do the worrying.' Impulsively she rang his office – something she wouldn't think of doing in normal circumstances.

'Selby and Leadbitter? Mr Joseph Selby, please. Out of his office? Well, put me through to Mr Jones, please.'

And it was from him she learnt that Joe was at Saxby's with Bob Withers, attending a site appointment with Melchester's chief planning officer and the city's engineer.

'An urgent matter, Mrs Selby? I will make the point when I ring up Mr Joseph at one o'clock. You will be at home? I'm sure Mr Joseph will be in touch within the hour . . . no trouble, I assure you . . . most happy to be of service.'

Good old Leadbitter. At least she knew he would find Joe and make the point. In the meantime, all she could do was to wait for Joe's return.

At Saxby's, in the big farm kitchen, the conference had ended and the four men were closing their briefcases. Joseph Selby and Bob Withers were well satisfied, having attained their main objectives. It had been agreed that the south side of the old house would now be fronted by a bar and dining accommodation, flanked on the east by changing rooms for men and women, each with access both to the bar and the course. At the west end of the extension the architect would provide secretarial offices and a card room. Mains electricity, already available, would be used for storage heating, drying rooms and cooking facilities, while the cart track from Melchester Court to the Melbridge–Melchester road would be resurfaced and main drainage installed. With the old house reserved for the professional golfer and his family, Joe and Bob agreed to the Water Authority's objection to the creation of an artificial lake. The Holmbrook would continue to wind its way across the course without diversion until it finally discharged its water into the Mel river. With a little judicious give-and-take, they had enjoyed a very successful conference.

At one o'clock Bob was already unloading a packed lunch provided by Melchester Court when the phone rang and Joe took the call from the office. It was Leadbitter Jones reporting to Mr Joseph . . . all quiet in the office . . . letters ready for signature . . . but Mrs Selby had phoned . . . wanted to see her husband most urgently . . . seemed a little agitated . . . gave no reasons . . . said she'd be at home all the afternoon.

There must be something wrong, very wrong indeed. But before he could ring his own number the city engineer was waiting to commandeer the phone with a sheet of papers. Joe made his apologies for leaving the party, but promised that within forty-eight hours his notes of the meeting would be circulated to those present. Only Bob Withers might have detected a hint of anxiety in the voice

of the suave professional solicitor with which Melbridge citizens were
so familiar.

Throughout the drive home, he tried to work out why Kathy
wanted to see him so urgently. Becky in a car accident? Danny
playing truant again? The last thing he expected was to find a woman
so preoccupied with her private anguish that she did not notice the
car's arrival nor the sound of his latchkey in the front door.

Suddenly, the words came bursting out.

'Oh, there you are, Joe, at last . . . Dear Joe, thank God you've
come . . . I must talk to you. I've got the most ghastly news . . . this
morning Oliver Carstairs has confirmed that I'm pregnant . . . baby
due in April next year . . . Joe, I'm terribly sorry . . . Joe, what are we
going to do? What do you want me to do?'

Kathy was sobbing and there was desperation in her staccato
phrases. Joe, for his part, was stunned into silence. Not for one
moment had he contemplated such an outcome to the love affair of
which Kathy had spoken so frankly. He recalled how their joint
confession – oh yes, he bore much of the blame – had been followed
by a reconciliation which had seemed to restore them to their earlier
and happier relationship. But now? They were faced with the grim
realities of Kathy's Lakeland madness.

Joe felt totally inadequate, wiping away his wife's tears, patting her
hands as if comforting a child who has fallen over. Could this be the
sympathy of silence which his father had prescribed as the best
antidote for grief? 'When seeking to share another person's sadness,'
he used to say, 'it's often better to keep silent until some banal
thought breaks the tension.'

Quite suddenly, inspiration came to Joe, as if old Isaac was
standing beside him.

'Do you know, Kathy, neither of us has had a bite to eat since
breakfast? You stay where you are while I go and make a pot of tea.'

While he waited in the kitchen for the kettle to boil, he fell to
wondering what advice his father would have given to a client facing
an unwanted pregnancy; and what Edward Baynes would have said.
In country communities babies are often conceived out of wedlock,
and parson and lawyer are more often consulted than people realise.
Of course, there was no parallel between the unsought pregnancy of a
thirty-eight-year-old married woman and boy-and-girl affairs which,

144

as often as not, lead to wedding bells and a happy life thereafter. But on one point Joseph Selby's mind was crystal clear. Neither of his mentors would have sanctioned an abortion except for overriding medical reasons.

He returned from the kitchen with a pot of Assam tea and a tin of McVities Digestive biscuits.

'Here's something we both need,' he said. 'After tea I'll pop across the Close to sign my letters and arrange to stay away from the office tomorrow. I'll be back within the hour. Meanwhile, try not to worry. We'll both think more clearly in the morning.'

22

That night Joe slept fitfully, plagued by a gaggle of dreams – struggles between Martin Wrattenley and Richard Fagg, an argument involving Dr Carstairs and the Professor – all of them pointless and inconclusive. Kathy, on the other hand, had taken a Mogadon and slept the night through. She was still only half awake when Joe roused her with her routine seven o'clock cup of tea.

'Changed your mind, Joe? Going to the office, as usual?' She looked up and then she saw him smile.

'Sorry, Joe, I should have known you'd keep your promise. You've got the day off and you've got a plan for it, haven't you? I can see it in your eyes. Out with it, Joseph Selby. Is it one of those little round tours like you used to plan with the children at Port Isaac?'

'Well, my dear, the BBC predicts sunshine and the trees will be showing their autumn colours, so I thought we might have a day out. What do you say?'

'Fine, Joe, fine.' She smiled up at him. 'I wouldn't mind betting that our outing includes a stop at Saxby's . . .'

Joe laughed. 'Right first time, Kathy. Let's call it a joint venture.'

By ten o'clock they were in the Rover and heading up the Melchester Road, Kathy having prepared a Thermos of coffee and Joe having bought a selection of fresh cut sandwiches from Tom Gutteridge's delicatessen in East Street.

They crossed the bridge over the half-completed Melchester bypass, and shortly after passing a warning to motorists to 'beware – heavy lorry exit', turned left up a farm track marked 'Saxby's Farm only'.

'This is where we start the round tour, Kathy. Soon that notice will be changed to read "Private road to Melbridge Golf Club".'

The track had been badly chewed up by heavy earth-moving equipment which could be seen in action to the right of them, but, at last, after a bumpy ride, the old farmhouse came into sight.

Joe assumed the role of official guide.

'This is where we alight, Mrs Selby. It is probably the last time you will be able to park outside Saxby's front door. To be specific, we are now standing on the site of Julian Grant's bar. Looking south, thirty yards to your left, you may like to imagine the eighteenth green. But now we start playing the course or, at least, the first nine holes.'

Joe's knowledge of the lay-out was only matched by his ignorance of how to play the 'royal and ancient' game – but he'd always been quick on the uptake and the three tours he'd taken with Julian Grant and the course architect had left him with a clear picture of the way the architect had incorporated the natural features of the landscape into his design.

Kathy began to respond to Joe's enthusiasm, as he slipped into a jocular guided tour patter.

'Each nine holes thirty-six par,' Joe was intoning, 'first and tenth holes easy par fours – we don't want members holding up play with lost balls. Each half includes two holes over five hundred yards long and two short holes ... pause for a moment, Mrs Selby ... here we are standing on the fifth tee. The green – two hundred yards away – will be on the far side of the Holmbrook. You will see that the player has to carry the stream. If he hooks, his ball goes into the copse over there – if he slices, his ball will disappear into the stream which, as you can see, twists up the right side of the green after crossing the fairway. It shows what a clever chap this golf architect is that Julian has commissioned ... I can even tell you that the second half of the course will contain two holes reminiscent of the seventeenth and eighteenth holes at Carnoustie ...'

'My dear Joe, your sales pitch is terrific.' Kathy was actually laughing.

'So what about a break for lunch?'

Now back at Saxby's, they laid a rug on the front doorstep of the old farmhouse, ate their sandwiches and drank their coffee.

'Next year,' said Joe, 'we should be able to sit in comfortable chairs on the club house terrace, watching other members finishing their matches on the eighteenth green.'

'So do we now play the second half of this figure-of-eight course reminding us of the Rye lay-out?' Kathy was pleased to be able to quote from Becky's information gleaned at the Feathers dinner party.

'No,' Joe decided. They'd done enough cross-country walking. It would be better to leave the second half for another day. But before leaving Saxby's, he led his wife to the back of the old farmhouse where builders were converting some outhouses into a professionals' shop. It was so placed that you would need to pass it whether you were starting your round at the first or the tenth tee.

'Now look, Kathy.' Joe had his back to the embryo shop and was pointing east. 'Here is our prize exhibit, which many courses would love to possess – a practice ground, stretching for seven hundred and fifty yards and running parallel with the first hole.'

'Joe, it's terrific.' She was looking east over the old grasslands, now cleared of hedges, to a point in the distance where a farm tractor was patiently chugging along, wide rollers on tow. 'You must be very excited.'

For the first time that day, Joe felt that his wife was sparking, genuinely responding to his enthusiasm.

'There's a long way to go yet, but I like to think we may be creating something that will, in God's good time, be enjoyed by a lot of people round here.'

Back in the car, they headed west along the track which led from Saxby's to the Home Farm. To their right were the fields which would one day contain the second nine holes. Somewhere in this corner of southern England, a series of bends in the Holmbrook would permit future golfers to play those two successive holes reminiscent of the famous finish at Carnoustie! Kathy in the passenger's seat was smiling. Dear Joe, he'd been such excellent company throughout the morning. She turned to look at him in profile, and was suddenly reminded of the day they'd driven to Melchester for the bypass enquiry. Since then, she'd taught him to drive, and a very good driver he'd become. But she knew that, at this moment, he was not concentrating on legal complexities nor yet on the potholes in the overused track.

'A penny for your thoughts, Joe.'

'Sorry. What's that you're saying?'

'Where's our next port of call, Joe? Are you going to visit your clients at Melchester Court?'

'No, Kathy. We'll leave them to themselves until we join them for dinner in two days' time.'

'So where are we going, then?'

They were crossing the private bridge over the bypass which Joe had persuaded the ministry to provide for the Melchester Estate, when he shook himself clear of his private thoughts or possibly his prayers. Kathy was never quite sure. But now he spoke.

'So sorry, Kathy, my mind was elsewhere. I've been thinking . . . please bear with me . . . I was thinking we've reached a point at which our round tour becomes a sentimental journey . . . or should we call it a pilgrimage?'

They had emerged from the Saxby's farm track to join the metalled road which connected Melchester Court with Holmesdale village. They drove past the ornamental gates giving entry to the overlarge Victorian mansion, and on past the Home Farm buildings and the cottages of those who worked at the Court.

Soon they reached the high ground, commanding a marvellous view of the valley and the Mel river. Ahead of them stood the church of St Wilfred's where, nineteen years previously, they had made their marriage vows. But they drove past the lychgate and were proceeding up the village street when Joe asked if Kathy would like to stop at Buckley's.

'No, thank you, Joe.' Kathy had guessed where the pilgrimage was leading. 'This is our day, yours and mine. I'd rather stay with you.'

And so they drove past Kathy's parents' house and past Joe's old home, until they left the car beside the old Methodist burial ground.

It was a lonely place – a small plot of land given freehold to the Methodists by a pious farmer in the early nineteenth century. The little redbrick chapel which had never seated more than fifty people now had the sad look of a place long closed to worship. The door was locked and so was the gate in the low wall surrounding the plot. But Joe and Kathy, leaning against the wall, were able to look down on the flat granite stone which marked Isaac Selby's grave. Miraculously, it was well cared for, the surrounding grass freshly mown and the stone edged by a border of newly planted wallflowers. 'Something my mother still remembers,' murmured Joe, and then they fell silent.

In that solitary place, both of them were aware of a strange experience . . . a new communion with each other and with the past . . . a new sense of communion, perhaps, with a merciful God whose love is timeless. Kathy found she was repeating to herself a snatched line from Psalm 46: 'Be still then and know that I am God.'

After those minutes of silence and contemplation, they simultaneously turned to each other.

'Well, Joe, what would Isaac think of me?'

'Your guess is as good as mine, darling. But one thing is certain. He loved you and Becky and Daniel with a great love. I think he would welcome an additional grandchild. Probably his only doubt would concern my ability to be a good substitute father.'

'What's that you're saying, Joe? You're ready to accept the baby as yours?'

'Why, certainly, if you will let me.'

Kathy looked at Joe and saw the little half-smile which meant so much. Her brown eyes shone with tears of relief as she clung to him.

'Oh, thank you, Joe,' she said. 'You really are a darling man. I'm so glad I married you.'

They walked back to the car, each of them ready to face their future. They had settled their problem. There would be a late addition to their family.

They returned down the hill from Holmesdale village to the ancient bridge which had given Melbridge its name. Both remembered it as the hill where Joe had once insisted on pushing Kathy's bicycle. The days of their courtship were not really so far away.

They re-entered 10 Ockenham Drive to find two letters on the doormat delivered by second post – one from Canterbury and one from Preston. It almost seemed as if Becky and Daniel had also participated in their parents' sentimental journey.

23

They opened Becky's letter first. It was typical of their daughter –
practical, bold handwriting, informative, no words wasted.

> The university brilliant . . . all modern buildings . . . lots of
> space . . . two friends from Melchester High in the same hall of
> residence as I'm in . . . named after T. S. Eliot . . . one of them
> doing sociology like me . . . everybody's very friendly . . . dance
> next week . . . must stop now . . . hope Dad's golf course is
> taking shape . . . Love Becky.

Danny's was also informative, but covered far more pages and
dodged about from topic to topic without any apparent logical
sequence.

> Saturday . . . had a terrific day with the CSM – took me along to
> Deepdale to see his team . . . we won 3–1 (I mean Preston
> North End won) . . . sat in what they call the pavilion seats
> where the Sergeant Major has lots of friends . . . but there's
> plenty of standing room in the terraces . . . used to be packed
> full when we were in the first division . . . that was in 1961 when
> Tom Finney was still playing for us . . . he's retired now but in
> Preston he's better known than the Mayor – or so the CSM
> says.

At this point there was a break for high tea, but the writer had
returned to his task, fortified by Rosie Harbottle's bubble and squeak
and provided with a refill for his ballpoint.

Where was I? Oh yes, with the CSM . . . actually he's why I'm writing . . . the Army expected the lads to write home once a week, he said. Hint, hint . . . OK I told him, I'll do the same, so here we go . . .

And on went Daniel Selby's letter, moving from Preston's earlier fortunes in the first division and their Cup win in 1938 to the excellence of Rosie Harbottle's cooking and his conviction that Lancashire high teas should be introduced into Melbridge life . . .

The writer suddenly switched to school life . . . no troubles about work, many of the textbooks the same as at Highminster, size of form about the same too . . . they all laughed at the way he talked . . . but he'd made them laugh too with his Podolski sketch and he had other impersonations in mind . . . the Prof. might be worried at a sketch he was working on – 'Elton John Selby in love with a microphone' but Rosie, his captive audience, said it was a real hoot . . . 'Mind you, Mum, she finds a lot to laugh at in spite of her legs getting tired . . . carrying too much weight . . . I think I might like to give her one of Mr Bailey's rocking chairs like President Kennedy's . . . More, much more next week. Much love from Lancashire and your son, Danny.' Under the flourish of a signature was a significant postscript: 'Am learning to play the clarinet . . . could be useful in a danceband. D.S.'

Kathy and Joe were both laughing as they reread Danny's report from Preston. Clearly the boy had settled well into his new life.

'So far, so good,' Joe was always cautious.

'We never had a letter like that from Highminster,' said Kathy. 'But when, Joe, should we tell them about the baby?'

It had seemed comparatively simple in the solitude of the old burial ground above Holmesdale after Joe had, without hesitation or any hint of self-righteousness, assumed the role of father. But this private resolution would have to go public some time. Who should be told what, and when?

'When in doubt, do nothing. We've certainly set ourselves a few problems,' he said, 'but I reckon the best thing we can do at this moment is to sleep on our worries . . . leave them alone for twenty-four hours. It's strange how often problems solve themselves, if given a little time in storage.'

In bed that night Joe brought his wife up to date on the set-up at

16

Melchester Court where they would be dining in a day's time.

He began with the present Earl: small of stature, expensively educated, average ability; no interest in farming problems, although inheriting a great estate in rich farming country; chief hobbies horseracing and fast cars. As a young man, he had probably spent too much time and money in London, where he had met and married Gloria Dunstable-Browne, the present Lady Melchester.

Gloria, it seemed, was no aristocrat, just one of two children born to a plain Mr William Brown, clever garage hand who had risen very fast in the Second World War. Drafted into REME, he'd risen to command a tank recovery unit in the Western Desert. After the war, Major Brown MBE had developed two splendid moneymaking businesses – secondhand cars and retread tyres – and then married a lady with strong social ambition which resulted in Bill Brown changing his name by deed poll to Major William Dunstable-Browne. He'd died in the sixties – an able, likeable man with a gutsy sense of humour, who often laughed at the prestige he'd gained from gratifying his wife's desire for a hyphenated surname. She too was dead, leaving two children, Gloria and Arkley, as joint heirs of a considerable fortune.

'And what of Gloria and Arkley?' Kathy was getting interested. Tales of the present Earl's rackety youth had been part of her upbringing on the Melchester estate. But Gloria and Arkley were less-known quantities.

'No comment,' replied her husband, with a wry grimace.

'You can't leave it like that, Joe. Let me put the question another way – what does Bob say about Gloria and Arkley?'

'Well Bob's got to be discreet, but I guess he shares the views of everybody else at the Court. In simple terms, Lady Melchester doesn't fit the part!'

It was clear that Gloria had no liking for country life and loved the fashionable London scene which Freddy had given up long ago. Equally, she took no interest in the colourful world of horseracing where Freddy Melchester found friendship and excitement. She hadn't been seen for years at Wincanton or Salisbury; and the smooth running of the Court staff was left to the old cook, Mrs Mullins, and the ultimate authority of Bob Withers.

'So why,' asked Kathy, 'is she involved in staging a dinner party for

Mr and Mrs Joseph Selby?' She looked at Joe's pursed lips, and smiled.

'Not a word, Joe. Your silence tells all – you are acting on Grandpa Selby's advice which you passed on to me years ago: "If you can't speak well of a man, say nothing." But I bet it's to do with Gloria's brother. Right?'

Joe wouldn't be drawn further. He professed to know nothing of Arkley Dunstable-Browne except that he was a half-commission man, playing a lone hand in the City. Bob Withers had been wary of him ever since he'd persuaded Freddy, who was a 'name' at Lloyds, to move from an experienced agent to a new and more adventurous set-up. So far, Arkley's advice had brought excellent returns, but Bob's City friends had suggested that Mr Arkley Dunstable-Browne was more interested in his own commission earnings than in conserving his brother-in-law's inheritance.

So why had Arkley persuaded his sister to ask a Melbridge solicitor and his wife to dinner? Kathy instinctively sympathised with Bob Withers. Who wouldn't be nervous of a man who sported such a preposterous name as Arkley Dunstable-Browne?

24

It was a warm night in early October, with the silhouette of the great house still visible as the Rover, driven by Joe Selby, breasted the final slope of the long drive up to Melchester Court. During the journey from Melbridge, driver and passenger had hardly spoken, both of them nursing their own thoughts, a mixture of excitement and apprehension.

Kathy was silently praying that she wouldn't let Joe down. She knew that this invitation was a big event in her husband's life, the culmination of an ambition which her imagination traced back to the day when Joe's father had stopped him from sitting for an Oxford scholarship. She was distinctly nervous of Lady Melchester but had taken heart from Joe's approval of her new dress.

'Exactly right,' he'd said before they had left Ockenham Drive. 'Suits you perfectly . . . you look great.'

As for Joe, the occasion was a milestone on the road which, starting with the Melchester Bypass Inquiry, had reached a point where he had gained the trust of the county as well as the citizens of Melbridge. He was apprehensive only to the extent that he would be meeting the formidable Lady Melchester for the first time, and her brother, whom Bob Withers did not like.

Joe parked the car in the forecourt, and with Kathy beside him, her shoulders protected by the smart little jacket which matched her evening dress, he was walking towards the front door when Bob Withers met them.

'Last minute briefing,' he said. 'I'm sure the ghastly Arkley wants to horn in on the golf course project. It's up to you, Joe, to keep him off the grass. OK? Right, so in we go.' And Bob tugged the bell-pull.

The imposing front door was opened by the cook's smart young daughter, Susan, dressed up as a parlourmaid for the evening, and she ushered them into the library to the right of the hall.

The anonymity of black dinner jackets could not entirely disguise the characteristics of the male members of the party. Lord Melchester, the youngest of them and the smallest in stature, welcomed Kathy and Joe with a charming smile and asked Bob to get busy with the drinks. The next senior in age was Arkley Dunstable-Browne, who was sipping a whisky and looking much older than his years. His open dinner jacket suggested a man who was clearly overweight and probably taking too little exercise. He contrasted unfavourably with the two older men: Bob Withers, tall and easy of approach and Joe, more muscular in build with strong features which gave no hint of what he might be thinking.

The two women showed up in more obvious contrast. Lady Melchester, taller than Kathy, was dressed more for a first night in the West End, but she was undeniably good looking and wore a truly beautiful diamond pendant. Mrs Joseph Selby's dark green and primrose dress emphasised the warmth of her suntanned arms, her lively eyes and the natural wave of her auburn hair.

While Bob was doing the rounds with the sherry, Joe quietly took stock of the company. It is surprising how much information the half hour of pre-dinner drinks can yield to a guest endowed with good hearing and inquisitive eyes. Joseph Selby, standing alone, heard His Lordship making sure that Kathy was happy with the pale dry Fino ('not so dry, Mrs Selby, as some of the sherry they seem to prefer in London, but Bob has an Amontillado to hand if you'd prefer it').

Across the room, he noticed that Arkley had swallowed his whisky, refused the sherry, and was busily mixing a dry Martini in a glass jug large enough to provide for 'the same again'. Joe thought he heard Bob say with a touch of asperity, 'For heaven's sake, Arkley, stop worrying about your blasted vintage port. My father taught me how to decant Dow's 1908 when I was a boy of fourteen.' But whatever Bob said was lost as Lady Melchester told her brother in her masterful voice to get a move on as she was tired of waiting for her Martini.

By the time dinner was served, Joe had come to certain conclusions: first, that Bob was not the right person to handle Arkley;

secondly that Arkley, to whom he had spoken briefly, was the sort of man who gambled with other people's money rather than his own; thirdly, that Lady Melchester shared no common interests with her husband. The only question mark in his mind concerned Arkley's relationship with his sister – was it possible that some of his stock exchange tips had failed to meet Gloria's expectations?

The fine mahogany table was really too large for six people. It meant, in effect, that two separate conversations tended to develop, between Freddy Melchester at the head of the table, with Kathy on his right and Bob Withers on his left, while Gloria at the far end was flanked by Joe and Arkley. The light from two silver candlesticks gave a glow to the polished surface and a sparkle to the silver, as the party sat down to a first course of salmon mousse.

Joe Selby, who had sipped orange juice before dinner, accepted a glass of the white wine offered by Bob Withers.

Arkley noticed and said, 'So you're not a total abstainer, Selby. I hope you'll appreciate the Chassagne-Montrachet . . . I was fortunate enough to buy at one of those forced sales set up to raise money for death duties . . .'

'That's nonsense,' Lord Melchester broke in, anxious to save Joe embarrassment, 'this wine was supplied by Gutteridge's in East Street and so was the claret for the main course.'

Freddy chuckled, and turned with a puckish smile to Kathy – 'Sorry to break in like that, Mrs Selby, but honour where honour's due. Years ago, when the 4th Earl was living here old Gutteridge decided to develop his wine department and recruited a sommelier made redundant when a West End hotel was sold to property developers. Cunning old Gutteridge appreciated that this character had a fine taste for wine and close contact with some of the best shippers in Bordeaux and Gutteridge's reputation for fine wine continues. I doubt whether there is a more reliable vintner in the south of England.

'But tell me more about your family. I really know so little about them.'

Kathy found her host a good listener. When she told him of Danny's lorry-hop to Preston and the subsequent change in the educational plans, her companion remarked that he wished he'd had the courage to do the same. Kathy gathered he took little pleasure in carrying out the duties which his inherited title imposed on him. He admitted, however, to getting involved in local affairs from time to time as, for instance, in a concert organised for Polish relief. 'And that is when I heard your boy playing the violin part in Beethoven's Archduke. What a talent he must have. And now you tell me that old Podolski was the teacher who spotted his potential. You must be proud of him.'

By the time the crown roast was being served, Kathy had agreed to accompany Freddy Melchester to the next race meeting at Wincanton.

'Never been there, my dear? A serious lapse in your education . . . we must put it right at once . . . jumps, you know . . . always attracts a good field . . . only thirty miles away and the steward's car park causes no problem . . . excellent dining-room and boxes with a splendid view of the course . . . Make it November? It's a date.'

At the other end of the table the conversation was concerned with more serious matters. Unabashed by his brother-in-law's intervention, Arkley was firing probing questions at Joe Selby, with scant respect for his sister sitting between them.

He opened with a sighting shot.

'Insurance, Selby, you say your clients are only concerned with house and car questions? Well, I'm glad to say I persuaded Freddy to leave the old stick-in-the-mud Lloyds agency his father used and move to a more enterprising lot in whom I have great confidence.'

Joe diplomatically agreed that Lloyds was a great institution but he doubted whether he would advise clients to stake the total value of their property as part guarantee against possible losses. He turned to try to involve Lady Melchester in the conversation, but Arkley overrode him.

'Nothing venture, nothing gain, eh?'

'Not exactly. But in matters of finance, I was brought up to the old principle of Polonius – "Neither a borrower nor a lender be."'

Lady Melchester joined the argument.

'I understand Mr Selby's point exactly. Our father began life as a garage mechanic and came from a very different background from Mr Selby's but he also observed the same rules. "Cash on the nail" was his ideal and he would have been wary of a system where you have to wait three years before you can measure the success of your trading.'

'My dear Gloria,' Arkley began, but decided to move to a subject of more immediate interest. 'So what about this golf course venture of yours? A bigger risk than insurance, eh?'

'Hardly my venture,' Joe registered a mild protest. 'But His Lordship believes that an eighteen-hole course is badly wanted by people in these parts. I walked the course two days ago with my wife and we were most impressed by the architect's skill in using the terrain's natural features, and the speed with which the earth-shifting tasks are being carried out. Do you play yourself? A £10,000 investment . . .'

'No time, I'm afraid . . . too many irons in the fire. But I might be able to drum up some financial support. You never know, do you?'

'No, you never know,' the Melbridge solicitor warily agreed. 'Why not have a word with Julian Grant? I'm sure you know the name?'

'A man with an eye to the main chance, what?'

'I wouldn't know,' Joe replied without betraying his growing distrust of the man across the table. 'My own opinion is limited of course by a solicitor's outlook, but I fancy that most people are motivated by what you call "an eye to the main chance", only some of them control this natural urge better than others.'

The crème caramel or fresh fruit salad had been served and enjoyed when Lady Melchester rose from the table to leave the men to sample Arkley's vintage port and probe deeper into the cost of constructing a golf course. She, at least, had understood the implied rebuke in the voice of the Melbridge solicitor and liked him the better for it.

Kathy had enjoyed every moment of her evening but was more than ready to join her hostess for the coffee awaiting them in the library. In the last few minutes she had been conscious of a pain in her left shoulder – resulting perhaps from her walk with Joe at Saxby's – but unaccountably it caused her to feel a need for air.

She was on the point of accepting a cup of coffee served in exquisite Crown Derby when she realised she must sit down. Mumbling apologies she backed away from the coffee table looking desperately for a seat. She managed to stagger to the edge of a settee before she collapsed in a dead faint – the only casualty being a standard lamp which crashed to the floor and caused its powerful light bulb to explode.

Lady Melchester called Joe from the dining-room. Susan, who had been clearing the plates from the table, rushed to the kitchen for Mum who arrived to take charge, complete with smelling salts and a large dishcloth.

'Loosen her skirt, Susan. Lift her feet on to the couch and hold that bottle close to her nose. Open a window, sir, it's air they need on these occasions,' and Mrs Mullins began to flap the dishcloth as if she was a 'second' in a boxing ring.

Slowly Kathy opened her eyes, looking dazed in these strange surroundings until she saw Joe.

'So sorry, Joe, so very sorry . . .'

Briskly, Gloria Melchester took practical charge. 'Your wife took quite a crack on the head just now, Mr Selby. You may think it wise for her to check in at the hospital on your way home.' And for his own reasons Joe was grateful to accept this brusque but wise advice.

A phone call briefed Matty Broadbent to expect them and Dr Carstairs was called too. Profuse apologies were tendered for breaking up the party and Bob Withers brought his estate car to the front door, so that, with a lowered passenger seat, Kathy could be in reasonable comfort on a layer of blankets and pillows.

Joe was about to hop into the estate beside Kathy when Freddy Melchester stopped him.

'Leave me your car keys, Selby. I'll follow you to the hospital. You'll be wanting your car afterwards and Bob can drive me back to the Court. No trouble at all, I assure you.' There was real sympathy in his voice. And then, with a conspiratorial smile on his face he added, 'Let Arkley finish the decanter. In my view, he paid too much for it.'

25

Matty and Oliver Carstairs were waiting at Melbridge hospital when the Ford estate drew up at the hospital entrance, closely followed by Freddy Melchester in the Selbys' Rover. Joe helped Kathy out of the car – a matter of courtesy rather than necessity, for his wife, although still looking white and frail, had made some sort of recovery, and was querulously asking why she wasn't being taken straight home to Ockenham Drive. There was nothing wrong with her, she protested . . . just terribly sorry to have been so silly and put an end to the party on which Joe set such store . . . but these things happened sometimes, so why all this fuss?

Dr Carstairs, however, took firm control. It was time, anyway, for him to give Kathy a routine check, and everybody would sleep more soundly if she stayed overnight in the single room which Matron had made ready for her. Perhaps Joe could help by driving home and fetching his wife a nightie, washing-things and something to wear in the morning. Meanwhile, he'd take her blood pressure and check her pulse.

Within the hour, Bob Withers and Lord Melchester had returned to the Court and Kathy was sleeping peacefully in her own nightdress. But Oliver Carstairs stayed for a further word with Joe and Matty.

'You were quite right to bring your wife here,' he told Joe. 'Her blood pressure is unusually low – 95/60 mm/Hg – and she has a raised pulse rate. She has also told me something that she may have been trying to conceal, namely that she's worried by a pain in her left shoulder. I don't want to sound alarmist but my snap examination suggests that these symptoms are connected with her pregnancy. I don't believe for a moment that the fainting at Melchester Court was caused by an overheated room or by the comparatively simple meal which she seems to have enjoyed.

'Luckily, James Messenger will be visiting Melbridge tomorrow. He's the gynaecological consultant at Melchester General, Joe, and enjoys a fist-class reputation. We'll ensure that he makes Kathy his top priority. There's nothing more to be done tonight. But, Matron, if Kathy complains of any pelvic pain of a cramplike nature or if she suffers any vaginal bleeding you must let me know. I'm free of surgery duties tomorrow, so I'll be here at eleven o'clock to meet James Messenger. And now it's high time we were all in bed. Goodnight, Matron. Goodnight, Joe. I'll keep in touch.'

Next morning, Matty telephoned Selby & Leadbitter to ask if Mr Selby could come to the hospital at his earliest convenience to meet the Melchester consultant. By one o'clock, decisions were being made on the strength of the consultant's diagnosis which, in fact, confirmed Dr Carstairs' fears. It was eight weeks since Kathy's last period and, by some mischance, she was suffering from an ectopic pregnancy. Put simply, as Mr Messenger explained, it meant that the foetus was growing in a fallopian tube. In such cases a laparotomy was essential: that is to say, an operation under general anaesthetic which removes the offending fallopian tube and allows the surgeon to clear the blood from the abdominal cavity. It would mean losing the baby and the consultant understood all too well the parents' disappointment. But Mrs Selby should make an uninterrupted recovery and the surgeon would look at the other fallopian tube. He could at least promise that if this was undamaged, the patient's fertility would not be affected.

Joe and Kathy accepted the inevitable. No other option seemed open to them. Within the hour Kathy was on her way to Melchester General Hospital where, on that same evening, a laparotomy was carried out by Mr Messenger.

Just before the anaesthetic took effect, Kathy was heard to say, 'Dear Joe, please tell the children what is happening.' And leaving messages for them was his immediate preoccupation.

Becky rang back from the university the same evening. 'Very sudden, wasn't it? No idea . . . how is she? Out of the anaesthetic? In

Melchester General for ten days at least? Gosh, Dad, I'm sorry . . .
darling Mum . . . Tell you what . . . I'll get compassionate leave . . . of
course, it'll be OK. Can't have you trying to look after yourself . . .
must stop . . . all my news when I get home . . . love . . .'

The phone went dead – coins had run out – but Becky's reaction to
the crisis had exactly followed the pattern Joe and Kathy would have
expected: shock, genuine sympathy followed by practical decisions
and no pointless questions. Joe hung up the phone, thanking God for
giving him such a lovely and predictable daughter.

Now for the unpredictable member of the family. Joe put in a call
to Preston, only to learn from Rosie Harbottle that Danny would be
out late . . . some concert party dress rehearsal, she believed. So
would Rosie please break the news to Danny next morning?

'Tell him not to worry, Mrs Harbottle. It's a difficult operation but
the surgeon is confident that Mrs Selby will make a complete recovery
. . . yes, a longish convalescence I'm afraid . . . but tell him his mother
will be back home well before he returns to Melbridge for the
Christmas holidays. And how is the boy?'

Danny was thriving. 'Friends everywhere, Mr Selby, always near
the top of the form, as you know, but finding time for out-of-school
activities, dance music and his clarinet . . . giving piano lessons to a
Barbadian neighbour's daughter . . . last Saturday he persuaded Mr
Harbottle to drive us to Keswick to meet a friend of his, a Mr Bailey,
that's it . . . It was a lovely day out.'

Rosie checked the flow of words to say how sorry she was to hear
about Mrs Selby and hoped Danny would not be too upset when she
told him the news.

When morning came Danny's reaction was dramatic. Rosie
listened to the boy trying to keep his emotion under control, as he
rang his father before going to school. But finally unable to suppress
some deep and hidden obsession within him, suddenly the words
came tumbling out.

'It's about a baby, isn't it, Dad? Something's gone wrong, I know
. . . I know. Let me explain. I've been working on a variation to a
Cumbrian cradlesong which I picked up from Mr Bailey. It was the
prettiest of melodies with a waltz rhythm, and I know exactly how the
theme could be developed. But somehow nothing would work out.
The happy major key wouldn't behave itself, the waltz rhythm of a

cradle lullaby became solemn and sad . . . d'you understand, Dad? I sort of knew in advance . . .'

'Yes, Danny, I understand. So will Mum.' Joe sought to reassure the boy. 'Try to keep calm. Remember the surgeon has promised Mum a full return to health. And don't be afraid to talk about our worries to Mr and Mrs Harbottle. They, too, will understand. As for Mum, you'll help her most by sending your next weekend letter direct to her in Ward B, Melchester General Hospital. Take her away from hospitals and operations and tell her about your concert party and your trip with the CSM to Mr Bailey. Now, off you go to school. 'Bye for the moment and be sure I'll let you know how Mum gets on.'

Joe put down the phone. He must get some sleep but first he forced himself to make a series of essential phone calls: to Leadbitter Jones, to Liz Hardingham, to Edward Baynes, to Bob Withers – and would he pass on the news about Kathy to His Lordship.

Then he sank back in his chair, the phone not securely replaced but dangling at his feet, his eyes closed. Strange how desperately sad he was at the loss of this child – sad for himself as well as for Kathy. He was oppressed by the knowledge that his decision to accept the fatherhood of Kathy's child had been pointless. He felt humiliated by the rejection of his offer – a sacrifice spurned. He was angry with God.

So he fell asleep. Nothing roused him until the late afternoon when Becky arrived from Canterbury, crept into the house and gently kissed her father on the forehead.

26

It was the seventh day since Kathy's operation, and Joseph Selby was using it to catch up with his office work. Becky, who had taken over the domestic duties at Ockenham Drive the moment she'd reached home from the university, had also arranged that she and her father should make the journey to Melchester General on alternate days – 'much less tiring,' she'd said, 'for Mum to talk with one visitor at a time, and much easier for the visitor, too.'

So Joe had spent the morning at his office on Southside. Now, with his desk clear, he was waiting for a surprise caller and speculating as to why Lady Melchester should have asked for this eleven thirty appointment.

Deciding that guessing was pointless, he abruptly rose from his desk chair and took a few paces towards the tall, stately window from which, two years previously, he had admired the view across the Close.

The view had not changed. October might have caused more leaves to fall from the oaks and chestnuts, but the church of St Peter and St Paul still dominated the scene, the irregular pattern of Melbridge rooftops charmed the eye, and a solitary pedestrian was hurrying across the Close on the diagonal path from Selby's Pavement to the Feathers in West Street.

Only two years ago! Joe looked back to the accumulation of hope and success which had led to the acquisition of these fine offices: his own sense of freedom following his father's death, the start of the Melchester Court connection ... and then, as if to square the accounts, he recalled his fateful decision to employ Richard Fagg.

Joe's balance-sheet mind raced relentlessly forward to look at what had happened since those halcyon days ... the failure of the Highminster experiment, the uncertainty about Danny's future, his own neglect of Kathy in order to help the wretched Fagg, and its consequences. Did this succession of setbacks stem from aiming too high, part of some counterweight process of nemesis?

Joe shook his head as if waking from a nightmare. No, he refused to accept the fatalism of the Greek philosophers. Could he not itemise a number of compensating factors to balance the account? Kathy's decision to come back to Melbridge, for instance ... their joint agreement to keep the baby and face the future head on, the happiness of Danny in Preston and, always at hand in a crisis, the presence of his pretty, dependable daughter. He smiled as he thought of Becky carefully listing the names of the friends who had sent Kathy flowers and get-well cards. His smile grew wider as he remembered Becky's special note concerning a package from Lord Melchester delivered by Tom Gutteridge. Only yesterday he and Kathy had celebrated the all-clear report from Mr Messenger by sharing the contents – a pot of pâté de foie gras, Bath Oliver biscuits, two peaches and a half bottle of Bollinger. What would Rachel Selby and Flora Pennington say? What indeed would his father have thought? He could only plead that a small relaxation of Puritan rules was a fair price for a strictly brought-up solicitor to pay if he was to number the aristocracy among his clients.

Joe was back at his desk as Gloria Melchester was announced. He rose to welcome her.

'And to what do I owe this pleasure, Lady Melchester?'

'A whim, Mr Selby, a whim. I require some legal advice, you see, and I remembered your offices were only a few steps away from the bank where I was meeting the new manager ... so here I am.'

Lady Melchester paused for a moment to look round the room.

'A very well-appointed office, Mr Selby,' her low pitched voice pronounced judgement, 'and a pleasant change I must admit from the dusty hovel where my London solicitor conducts his business ... is Mrs Selby responsible for the décor?'

'No, Lady Melchester, I left everything except the price to the excellent Mr Higgins of East Street.'

In spite of her masterful contralto voice, the lady was finding it hard to come to the point.

'Alas,' she said, 'I come to Melbridge so rarely that I've developed an obsession that people always wonder what I'm doing here – the bank staff, for instance, or your people in the general office downstairs . . .'

'And you think they will be asking themselves and each other why Lady Melchester should be calling on a Melbridge solicitor?' Joe answered the unspoken question.

'May I suggest that we gratify their curiosity by letting it be known that you have come to inquire about my wife's operation?'

'Make it known, Mr Selby?' Gloria was puzzled.

'We phone Melchester Court to instruct your chauffeur to wait for you in the Feathers car park.'

'The Feathers, Mr Selby?'

'Where I would suggest you take lunch with me, Lady Melchester.'

'Mr Selby, I have to admire the way you think on your feet. I suppose that's why I'm calling on you today. You see I liked the way you gave the old "one-two" to my brother the other evening.'

'You mean?'

'A straight left to the midriff when you turned down Arkley's insurance proposals; and the upper cut with your right to the jaw when you told him – oh so tactfully – that neither you nor Julian Grant needed his financial help for your blessed old golf course venture.'

Lady Melchester relaxed while Joe altered the arrangements for the chauffeur and reserved a table.

'And now, Lady Melchester, tell me how I can help.'

Her answer was explicit. She had decided that her marriage was hopeless – going from bad to worse – total incompatibility, Mr Selby. She couldn't stand country life; much less hotted-up cars and horseracing, while Freddy felt like a fish out of water among her London friends. Their only hope lay in getting clear of each other.

Joe Selby pursed his lips. He was equally explicit. He feared he could not take instructions in the case presented to him. This was a matter for her own solicitor who would need to deal with Lord Melchester's family firm.

Lady Melchester took the point, but wouldn't let it rest.

'All I want you to do, Mr Selby, is to expound to me the state of the present laws on separation and divorce.'

'That is simply done,' said Joe and provided the information which would have been available at any public library oɪ Marriage Guidance Council. In '69 and '73 the divorce laws had been radically revised so that in 1976, if, in spite of their solicitors' best efforts to bring about a reconciliation, both parties were equally determined to separate, the two solicitors would be able to arrange a Deed of Legal Separation. There would be one basic condition that for two years there would be no meeting between the parties to the separation. Thereafter, a divorce would follow and be duly approved by the courts. Joe rounded off his resumé with some facts about the separated wife's tax advantages and Lady Melchester appeared well satisfied with his 'tutorial'. She smiled contentedly.

'So, Mr Selby, without making a positive recommendation, your interpretation of the law would suggest that if two people have made up their minds to end their marriage then, for Heaven's sake, take the quick and cheap course, and agree to start and complete the process without rancour or recrimination.'

Joe Selby smiled in turn.

'That would be your interpretation of my words, milady. But I can honestly say that, in my professional career, I've always tried to follow my dear old father's dictum that a good solicitor must be, first and foremost, a man of peace.'

At twelve thirty Joe Selby and his surprise visitor left the office. On the way out Mr Leadbitter Jones was informed in a clear voice that Lady Melchester had called to inquire about Mrs Selby's post-operative progress. He also understood that Mr Joseph would not be returning to Southside after lunch as he was due to meet Mr Julian Grant at Saxby's and tomorrow would be bringing his wife home to Melbridge.

There was no further legal talk as Lady Melchester and Joe Selby crossed Selby's Pavement to enter the Close for the short walk to the Feathers. The conversation ranged from the activities of the Selby children to the complexities of the golf club development. Lady Melchester was clearly delighted by her first visit to the Feathers and commented most favourably on Eleanor Grant's cuisine. But, after escorting his guest to her car, Joe was left wondering why she had called on him for advice? Was it really no more than a whim?

27

Joe was lucky enough to see James Messenger when he collected Kathy from Melchester. The consultant spoke with all the pride of a portrait painter after a final sitting – delighted to have pleased his client but equally pleased with his own handiwork.

'All clear,' he said. 'A model patient . . . but may I rely on you and Dr Carstairs to ensure that Mrs Selby takes her convalescence seriously – six weeks' rest and further six weeks of light exercise . . . no tennis tournaments, let us say, before next Easter.'

Such restrictions were not onerous. Becky felt able to return to Canterbury for the rest of the university term while Liz Hardingham and neighbours in Ockenham Drive looked after the shopping and cooking needs of the family. With Christmas approaching, Jack and Liz Hardingham would include the Selbys in their Christmas celebrations up at Holmesdale village.

In mid-December Danny returned from Preston for the holidays. His absence in Lancashire had never been a case of 'out of sight, out of mind' but his letter to his mother in hospital had projected him centre stage in Kathy's thinking.

The letter was a typical Danny performance – six pages long, people and incidents tumbling over each other, no logical sequence but sufficient references to Rosie and the CSM to convince his parents that he was totally happy in the Harbottle home.

Thus they learned how the CSM's gloom over Preston North End's mediocre results had been dispelled by the success of the visit to Mr Bailey's workshop near Keswick. Mention of Mr Bailey led back to Rosie Harbottle's rocking chair. To pay for it, Danny was relying on a letter from Jan Podolski which suggested that occasional fees could be expected from taking part in chamber concerts in south coast resorts during the summer holidays . . . Oh, and he was also earning fifty pence a week for giving piano lessons to the eleven-year-old daughter of a Methodist friend of Rosie – a skilled carpenter from Barbados. 'The girl is such fun to teach, Mum, all rhythm in her toes and fingers – but a broad Lancashire accent when she sings! I give her piano accompaniments for her Caribbean songs! Which reminds me,' the letter rambled on, 'I've had a letter from Ratty at Highminster. Sensation! Major Wrattenley has taken a job in Guyana to do with rainforest conservation and Ratty's flying to join him at Christmas – some chaps have all the luck!'

There was more, much more, to follow – the school in Preston, the concert he was running, the clarinet – but for the moment Kathy couldn't read another word. The joy, the grief, the tears were back as the letter dropped from her hand and she stared listlessly at the flowers and get well cards surrounding her bed.

She was still fighting the tears when her mother made a routine teatime visit.

'Poor darling,' Liz Hardingham said to herself, 'she's taking the loss of the baby very hard.'

A few days after Kathy's return to Ockenham Drive, Danny was again the subject of discussion – on this occasion in the coffee room of the Melbridge Club where Jan Podolski was often to be seen following his election backed by John Lucas and Harry Leng.

Joe Selby had dropped into the club for a quick lunch and was pouring himself a coffee when the Professor closed in on him.

Joining Joe for coffee, the old man proceeded to air his anxiety about the future of his favourite pupil.

'A word about your son, Mr Selby . . . I step where angels don't tread – Harry says not my business – but as artist and teacher am compelled to speak.'

Joe had no time to spare, but he liked the old man and replied, kindly enough, that he would be grateful if the Professor could say what he had to say in the space of the next five minutes.

'Golf club most urgent, eh?' The Professor smiled knowingly and came straight to the point.

'Mr Selby, sir, I ask you please to bring your son back to Melbridge for rest of schooling. You ask me why so anxious? I tell you, Mr Selby. Your son – I speak as expert teacher – possesses not only music genius but also very strong will. Danny not interested in high road to fame ... always practising, always journeying – New York, London, Paris, Tokyo, always aeroplanes, hotel rooms, critics – you understand? No, your most gifted son will prefer low road to happiness – make home, save others, doing good in slums, teach – who knows? But,' the Professor's hand clapped down on the table with an emphasis that made the coffee cups jump, 'Danny will still want to use music gift – perhaps teacher, composer, who shall say? Therefore, I beg you, Mr Selby, to ensure he gains necessary qualification, which is a degree at the Royal Academy.

'Apology, Mr Selby, for taking busy man's time. I only add Harry Leng and John Lucas at school agree, and they will welcome him back with the arms open.'

Jan Podolski paused for a moment. Then he rose from his chair, made a slight Continental bow and asked Joe to convey to Mrs Selby his best wishes for full recovery together with considered opinion of ancient Professor of Music, University of Cracow.

The two men left the club together and walked along Selby's Pavement as far as Joe's office. There they parted company and Joe watched the old man striding across the Close to catch the bus for Abbotshaven. Joe knew Podolski had spoken from a full heart and Joe knew that the old man was right.

Back at the office Joe switched his mind to the golf club project. It was so different from the problems which usually occupied his thinking. Normally he would be playing a solo part, using his legal knowledge to solve the problems or guide the actions of a variety of private clients. But in this matter of the golf club he was one of a quartet, each with a specific part to play. Or should he not now think of the team as a sextet since the course architect, Piers Bolder and Sandy MacNaughton, the newly appointed professional, must be added to the original participants – Lord Melchester, Bob Withers, Julian Grant and himself?

Tomorrow their plans would be public knowledge. As soon as the planning authority was satisfied, the project had been pushed into top gear. They had agreed on the simple title – the Melbridge Golf Club –

and a company had been formed allowing for ordinary shares and debentures to be held by its members. To use the jargon of the day, it would be a Members' Club.

The bank had made funds available to meet the first construction costs, but the financial requirement had been greatly eased by Lord Melchester's quixotic decision not to ask for any immediate payment for the land – Joe was still pondering whether the debt should be expressed as a seventy-five-year loan or as a debenture.

Moreover, the reconstruction of Saxby's farmhouse to form the club house and the provision of a professionals' shop for Sandy MacNaughton were being financed by Melchester Breweries who would hold the franchise for bar and catering.

So far, so good. Indeed, the autumn weather, aided by Bob Withers' enthusiastic workforce from the Home Farm, had allowed them to complete the build-up of subsoil and drainage for greens and tees. Luckily, the warm air of the southern counties had also permitted the sowing of grass seed late in the year.

So far, all had been done in faith. The sextet, advised by Julian and MacNaughton, had even agreed the terms of membership: £250 per annum for men and women, £350 for man and wife and special encouragement for original members to subscribe for ten-year membership – a very reasonable bargain, thought Joe, in the light of probable price inflation.

He sat back in his chair. The plans were laid. Tomorrow Julian Grant's publicity would begin – posters all over the place, a long article in the *Melchester Chronicle* and – hopefully – an exclusive story in the *Telegraph* about equal terms for men and women. Joe felt the anticipation and excitement of a soldier on the eve of battle. There was nothing more to be done. Or was there?

His mind flashed back to his schooldays and out came one of old Isaac Selby's favourite quotations. Something, wasn't it, from the Epistle of James?

'Faith, if it have not works, is dead.'

Joe's hand strayed to the desk drawer where he kept his cheque book and bank statements. A quick look at the cash on deposit, and he was writing a cheque for £7,500 in favour of the Melbridge Golf Club – £350 family membership, multiplied by ten, plus £4,000 for debentures and ordinary shares.

He left a few minutes later, waving a cheerful goodnight to the people in the general office.

'Mr Joseph sounds unusually perky this evening,' said Leadbitter Jones to the world at large.

28

The ladies of Melbridge displayed their usual curiosity about each other's medical condition, and in the normal run of things, the sudden nature of Kathy Selby's operation would have evoked sympathetic speculation at many casual East Street meetings or the mid-morning break at the lady cakemaker's.

'So sad about Kathy Selby – sudden emergency, my dear . . . Mr Messenger called in . . . taken ill, they say, at Melchester Court . . .'

But very soon the appearance of handbills announcing the formation of the Melbridge Golf Club provided a more fruitful topic of conversation which switched the Melbridge spotlight from Kathy to her husband.

Julian Grant's publicity men had done their work well, and Joe Selby watched the development of the campaign with all the fascinated excitement of a general staff officer watching his battle plans being translated into action in the field.

First came the simple notices stressing the name of the club and directing membership inquiries by post to Selby & Leadbitter, Southside, Melbridge, or by phone to a Melchester Brewery extension number or to the Professionals' shop at Saxby's. The handbills were to be seen all over the district: in the shops of Melchester, Abbotshaven and Melbridge, in the Public Library branches and pubs managed by Melchester Breweries – and, of course, in the Melbridge Club and the foyer of the Feathers.

But this handbill exposure was only the initial thrust. During January, February and March of the New Year, successive press releases were to announce the appointment of Sandy MacNaughton as Professional in Residence; next, the availability of the practice ground for members and prospective members; and, between Easter and Whitsun, the provision of bar service and snacks in the new club house. Finally, on 1 July, the eighteen-hole course would be open to members, using temporary greens and mats on tees.

Feature articles would also be carried by the *Melchester Chronicle* with the course architect, Piers Bolder, explaining how the natural features of the land had been incorporated in the design of the course, and Julian Grant showing how the old Saxby's farm buildings were being converted into the new club house.

But it was the *Daily Telegraph* diary piece which really excited Melbridge. A brief paragraph, commenting on the spate of golf courses being planned, reported that the picturesque old town of Melbridge was breaking new ground by forming a Members' Club in which men and women would have equal rights and pay uniform subscriptions. The writer paid generous tribute to the Earl of Melchester who had made the land available; and added a hint ('I am told on good authority') that the idea of equal status for women had first been mooted by a schoolgirl who had never played golf in her life.

Such national news – a mere two inches of type – might have been read by a million people and forgotten twenty-four hours later. In Melchester, Abbotshaven and Melbridge, however, it could be guaranteed a much longer life. There can be little doubt that in the early months of 1977 the formation of the Melbridge Golf Club became the main topic of conversation up and down the Mel valley, above all in Melbridge.

In the Melbridge Club, for instance, John Lucas let it be known that in addition to applying for personal membership he was hoping to negotiate some special arrangements for Old Melbridgians and for members of the present school. A question to Joseph Selby, who was tactfully asking him about Danny's possible return to the school, elicited the unequivocal reply that Joe considered the ten-year membership offer to be a good investment. At the Feathers bar Tom Gutteridge remarked that if that cautious old solicitor regarded ten-year membership a sound investment, it must be a good thing. It was rumoured that Dolly Hayward would be taking up the game again.

Old Leadbitter Jones who was in sole charge of the golf club file in the office on Southside, was as busy with membership inquiries as

Julian Grant's secretary at the brewery and Sandy MacNaughton in his newly equipped professionals' shop at Saxby's.

Not for years had Kathy seen her husband so happy. He'd seemed almost shamefaced when he'd first confessed to applying for a ten-year family membership, but she'd swept aside his doubts with her own enthusiasm.

She kissed him and put her arm round him. 'Well done, Joe,' she said. 'No ifs and buts. In for a penny, in for a pound. We give it a go, eh? And we go it together.'

There was still a month before she would be taking strenuous exercise, but on a warm January day, she accompanied Joe to inspect the progress being made on the second nine holes. As they crossed the Holmbrook short of the fifteenth green they shouted in unison: 'And those who are familiar with the great Scottish courses will be reminded of the famous finishing holes at Carnoustie.'

They laughed and were surprised to hear their laughter echoed by Bob Withers who emerged with another man from a clump of trees to inspect the state of the grass seed on the new green.

'Meet John Mullins,' Bob said, introducing his companion. 'He leaves this week for a greenkeeper's course before becoming the first member of the club's ground staff. John has always been in charge of the mechanical equipment at the Home Farm and now he's proved himself a wizard with the big mowing machines. That's why the practice ground is already open for play.'

Kathy and Joe left the embryo green committee and concluded their tour before turning from the site of the eighteenth green to go round the old farm buildings and approach the new professionals' shop. Out on the practice ground they could see the big familiar figure of Edward Baynes hitting ball after ball towards a white stake post about one hundred and fifty yards away.

Sandy MacNaughton came out of his shop to greet them.

'Ay, that's the vicar,' he said. 'A natural hitter of the ball . . . needs no help from me, though his congregation could help him lower his handicap with a set of new clubs . . . Those weapons he's using might fetch a good price at an antiques fair. The same would be true of Dr Latimer's set . . . which reminds me, sir, that the doctor has applied for the life membership option, as he's retired and over fifty-five.'

Sandy turned to Kathy.

'My apologies, Mrs Selby, for talking shop with your husband, but I've booked you for your first lesson in March: and your set of Jean Donald clubs has arrived. I look forward to our next meeting.'

'That Scotsman appeals to me,' Joe remarked as they drove back to Melbridge. 'Shrewd, you know . . . a salesman as well as a teacher . . . and very discreet too, judging by a story Bob told me about Christmas Day at Melchester Court.'

'Tell me more.'

'Well, it's a sad little story. Bob, you remember, was away with his parents in Devon and there was no Gloria for company, so His Lordship returns from the mid-morning communion service at St Wilfred's to eat a solitary lunch in that vast house – a slice of Fortnum's game pie, a glass of claret and a first dig at the Stilton, according to Bob. Anyway, after his lonely meal, our Freddy decides to take some exercise. Somewhere out on the new golf course he's caught in a sudden burst of rain . . . no shelter . . . soaked to the skin. But the eldest of the MacNaughton children spots him and soon His Lordship is drying out in the old farmhouse kitchen. Bob alleges that Sandy fitted him out with a Guernsey sweater and a rainproof windcheater before driving him back to the Court! But the point is that MacNaughton hasn't said a word about the incident to anyone. I like a man who can keep his mouth shut.'

'Poor Freddy,' said Kathy, as they closed the garage at number ten. 'Alone in that enormous house. Gosh, I feel sorry for him.'

Two letters, delivered by second post, were waiting for them on the mat inside the front door – one of them a large white envelope with bold handwriting and a London postmark addressed to Joseph Selby Esq., the other an airmail letter for Mrs Selby – name of sender: Wrattenley, P.O. Box 43, Georgetown, Guyana, South America.

Joe and Kathy opened their respective letters and then exchanged them.

Gloria's was straightforward – 'Thank you for the delightful hospitality at the Feathers and thank you for the clarity of your legal exposition which has been shared with Freddy. You will be pleased to know that there will be "no rancour, no recrimination". The address and telephone number of this notepaper will always find me, should you have cause to visit London, etc. etc.' ending with a signature spread across the page: 'Gloria Melchester.'

Martin's aerogram took up less space, but was more informative:

> Dear PS (I hope you will forgive my use of your chosen 'nom de plume'),
>
> I realise your letter requires no answer from this mad Englishman who has chosen to give up the peace and beauty of Lakeland in favour of a steamy rainforest in a forgotten corner of South America. Peter (who has been with me for Christmas) may well have told Danny about my move to this forestry job in Guyana (probably still showing in your atlas as British Guiana).
>
> Yet I feel you should know that I applied for this overseas job many months before you and Danny came to Rydal.
>
> Somehow, I'd lost interest in a routine inspectorate overruled by committees. I felt too full of life to relax in the peace and beauty of Lakeland. With Peter growing up (how fast time flies) the obligation to stay in England no longer seemed relevant.
>
> Mrs Gibbs will be free to open the house at Rydal to provide bed and breakfast for holidaymakers, but she will keep my rooms and workshop for Peter and me when I finally decide to 'hang up my boots'.
>
> Meanwhile, I do not forget (how could I?) the joy of your company in those lovely August days of 1976. They remain the more vivid for being remembered in a land where the natural wealth of our planet is being squandered and brings small comfort to the foresters who seek to 'buck the trend'.
>
> May all go well with you and your family in Melbridge – and please remember me most specially to Danny.
>
> Affectionately, as always
> Martin.

Joe handed back the letter to Kathy.

'So you won't tell him about the baby? It's better, you think, to leave that part of the story unspoken?'

'I think so, Joe ... yes, I think so.' Kathy clung to Joe as if for support. Then she added: 'We made our decision together, didn't we, beside old Isaac's resting place. Surely it's better for us to think of the lost baby as our grief – and ours alone.'

29

In Melbridge the warm spring days of 1977 seemed to make all things new. In the traffic-free, unhurrying centre of the little town you could see and feel the change – pedestrians stopping to pass the time of day on Selby's Pavement, or resting on one of the seats in the Close where the ancient trees were waking from their winter sleep.

Further afield, small gardens ablaze with forsythia and a profusion of daffodils gave way to early blossom in the orchards, and on the grammar school playing fields goalposts had disappeared and ground staff were busy preparing cricket pitches. On Easter Day, a peal of bells and the music of celebration had proclaimed the certainty of Resurrection from the great church of St Peter and St Paul.

To Joe and Kathy Selby the music and colour of spring swept from their minds the crises of the previous year – the joy and the grief, the exhausting sequence of repentance and sacrifice.

It seemed as if the pieces of the family jigsaw puzzle were falling into place.

Danny, who had taken back to Preston the Royal Academy of Music admission form, reported that the CSM considered it right for him to take his 'A'-levels from Melbridge and have the help of the Professor and Harry Leng for passing Grade Eight and preparing for the RAM audition. Dear Rosie had agreed, but of course she never disagreed with the CSM

'Not to worry,' she said. 'You'll be well remembered. When you're our age, you'll know that life is full of hello and goodbye. It's best if you treasure the friendship and forget the partings.'

Danny had also been cheered by a further visit to Mr Bailey

who had promised to deliver the rocking chair for Rosie during the summer Term, even if Danny still owed him a few pounds.

Then, one Saturday in early May, Becky turned up unexpectedly in Melbridge with a good-looking young man in tow.

'This is Jeremy Caxton,' she explained. 'He's the chap I met at a dance last term . . . wants to see Dad's golf course . . . knows that I was the schoolgirl mentioned by the *Daily Telegraph*.'

In the course of the frequent visits which followed this introduction, it transpired that Jeremy was the younger son of parents living in West Kent, that he had qualified as a solicitor, was at present working in the offices of a well-established Canterbury firm and lodging in a village nearby.

When the temporary tees and greens of the Melbridge Golf Club were opened for play, Jeremy arrived with golf clubs to play the course with Becky.

'We decided to play with one ball, as if we were foursome partners,' Becky explained airily. 'Easier that way, you see: and quicker too, and no lost balls. Actually, Jeremy plays from a single figure handicap on his home course . . . hits the ball a mile but thinks Sandy MacNaughton has given me a jolly good start.'

Nobody could mistake the symptoms. Jeremy and Becky were in love. The Selby family was growing up.

In the week when Jeremy made his first visit to Melbridge, Lord Melchester had tried to telephone Joe Selby at his home address. But the latter had already set off on his walk to the office, so Kathy took the call.

'Mrs Selby? Freddy Melchester speaking . . . sorry to bother you . . . a private matter for Joe . . . don't want to disturb him at his office . . . could you ask him this evening if he can spare me a couple of hours some time . . . next week . . . yes, out here at Melchester Court . . . shall we say next Tuesday ten o'clock, unless I hear to the contrary? Thank you so much . . . oh, one thing as we're talking . . . I'm looking forward to taking you as my guest to the Wincanton spring meeting . . . goodbye for now.'

Kathy added her own comments when she passed the message to Joe.

'Used your Christian name, sounded nervous, sort of jerky . . .

acting, I think, on a sudden impulse ... may want your advice, Joe, before making up his mind about something.'

And a very shrewd comment too, thought Joseph Selby when he kept his Tuesday appointment and listened to his host's story, sitting in the library at Melchester Court.

Freddy Melchester outlined very briefly how he had come into the title at the age of three. He paused with a wry smile. 'You will appreciate, Mr Selby, that in such matters a three-year-old boy has no choice?'

Satisfied that Joe was getting the point, His Lordship went on to explain that interest from the estate, carefully controlled by a London solicitor, had paid for his upkeep and education. While he was still at Eton his mother had remarried and was living in Scotland with her stockbroker husband and their three children. But at the age of twenty-one the young Earl had taken full possession of the Melchester inheritance.

There was a short diversion when Mrs Mullins entered the library with a percolator and asked His Lordship not to let the coffee get cold.

Freddy Melchester thanked her most courteously and turned again to Joe.

'So you are listening, Mr Selby, to a comparatively wealthy peer, lumbered with a title he doesn't want and a house that is far too large. And, since he and his wife have agreed to go their own separate ways, he realises that his local friends are, to all intent and purposes, limited to Bob Withers and the Mullins family.'

'So you and Lady Melchester have agreed to ask for a legal separation?'

'Yes, indeed, and we have each instructed our London solicitors to complete the job "without rancour or recrimination".'

Lord Melchester looked up at Joe, the same shy smile on his face.

'Your words, Mr Selby, which Gloria quoted to me with the utmost satisfaction. Let me add that I am equally grateful. You have, at least, suggested the swiftest and cheapest way to escape with dignity from a situation which had become intolerable.'

Joe Selby acknowledged the compliment.

'And you have some further plan in mind, Lord Melchester?'

Freddy Melchester laughed.

'First of all, Mr Selby, may I call you and your wife by your Christian names? And will you do the same with me?'

Seeing Joe's embarrassment, Freddy was quick to reassure him.

'I know it takes time to break with social conventions – it's taken Bob Withers a couple of years, but of course he's an employee of the estate. Try out the idea when, as fellow pupils of Sandy MacNaughton, we start playing golf together. But let us get down to more serious business.'

With growing excitement Joe listened to Freddy Melchester's plans.

First, Joe was instructed to handle an application to the planning authority for permission to convert derelict cottages and buildings on the estate 'to other use' – in other words, private houses.

Secondly, would Joe explore the possibility of selling Melchester Court to a school or institution or one of those companies which specialised in converting overlarge country houses into flats for retired people.

Lastly, he wondered whether Joe and Kathy would help him to give young Susan Mullins a chance to realise her potential. It was a shame to keep her among the Court employees – a clever girl, Joe ... a bagful of 'O'-levels, three good 'A'-levels from the new school at Abbotshaven ... about the same age as your daughter, I guess, but more interested in a business career than university ... He didn't know how to go about the task but Joe and Kathy would understand his wish to help the Mullins family after all their kindness over the years.

Joe had been surprised by Freddy Melchester's frankness and his heart was moved, his mind challenged by this young man whom he reckoned to be still under forty, who had trusted him with two very personal requests as well as two major business assignments.

Before taking his leave he promised to report back as soon as he had explored the property market and sounded out the chief planning officer in Melchester. He also felt sure that Kathy and Becky would have some good ideas about the right course for Susan Mullins. Although he could not quite persuade himself to use Melchester's Christian name, he did at least reciprocate the hope that the two of them might manage to fix up some golf when the new course was open for play.

* * *

Back in Ockenham Drive he answered Kathy's questions with honest enthusiasm.

'A truly delightful character, Kathy. He suffers from a title and status he never wanted, and that's left him shy and short of friends and confidence. But he's humble enough to seek our friendship and, by Heavens, I long to give him the help he needs.'

'And why not?' she replied, kissing and putting her arms round him.

'Well done, my darling. Between us, we'll help our Freddy to find a happier world.'

She left Joe, and prepared the evening meal. As she dished up she smiled. A new thought crossed her mind. Had she not also been listening to a man revealing himself? A slightly older man certainly: but one who had cast off the trappings of an ambitious, calculating lawyer and uncovered the generous sympathy of the true man she'd come to love twenty years ago.

30

In the second half of July, 1977, Danny came home. His summer term in Preston had started with the hard labour of eleven 'O'-level exams and ended triumphantly with a school variety concert in which he had been both compère and chief performer.

On the last Saturday of term, he and Bert Harbottle had collected the rocking chair from Mr Bailey and presented it to Rosie, complete with cushions of brilliant colours secretly bought and made up by Danny's Barbadian pupil and her mother. Inevitably, the gift had been made the excuse for a party – catering by Rosie, guests comprising a mixture of school and Harbottle friends, and entertainment spontaneous and unplanned, but memorable for Caribbean songs beautifully rendered by Danny's young music pupil and accompanied by him on the piano.

Finally, Danny used his powers of persuasion to good purpose with Bert Harbottle who had agreed to drive his young lodger home in his ten-ton diesel, Alexander the Great.

Dawn patrol, the CSM had ordered. 'Alexander will only make the detour to Melbridge if we guarantee to offload at Filton before 1400 hours and take on our return load at Avonmouth by 1700 hours.'

By making an early start, the CSM found the traffic at Preston comparatively light, and very soon Alexander was cruising down the M6 at a steady 65 mph.

'You're uncommon quiet this morning, Danny. Anything on your mind?'

'No, Sarge. I've just been enjoying the music of Alexander's wheels and making up a rhyme to fit the rhythm. Give me five minutes and I'll let you hear it.'

The CSM consulted the clock on the dashboard. 'Time's up,' he said. 'Let's be having you,' and Danny began to recite with relish what he called 'The Ten-Tonner's Dance'.

> Tootle the trumpet, rattle the drum.
> Alexander's thundering south.
> Wake up Melbridge, here we come,
> Heading for Filton and Avonmouth.

The beat was so insistent that soon the CSM was joining in too.

After Spaghetti Junction they moved south-east to join the 'A' road through Melchester. 'Time for you to take the map and guide me towards this one-horse town of yours,' Bert pronounced, 'and remember, son, that Alexander doesn't care for country lanes.'

Danny made no mistakes. They joined the east–west road and, short of Melchester, turned into the newly completed bypass. On their left Danny pointed to men and machines working on his father's new golf course. A few moments later they passed under the bridge that had been constructed to carry the heavy farm equipment from the old farmhouse to Melchester Court and, shortly after crossing the Holmbrook, reached the double bridge over the Mel river and the Melchester–Melbridge road which ran parallel with the river.

'Nearly home!' Danny shouted. 'Off the bypass now, Sarge, to join the Melbridge road. Watch for the school playing fields on your left, and then brake for turning right into our road. There, see it? By the bus stop.'

The hydraulic brakes were applied and Alexander turned majestically into Ockenham Drive – surely the biggest vehicle ever to enter that trim No Through Road of desirable residences. Best of all, Kathy and Becky were waving a welcome from the front gate.

Danny climbed down from the passenger seat and ran round the bonnet to receive the violin case reverently handed down by the CSM before rushing to greet his family. Could anyone but Danny have staged such a *coup de théâtre*?

In spite of their entreaties, Mr Harbottle would not stop for a meal. 'Just a bit of a leg stretch, Mrs Selby, and a quick cuppa if you can fix it.' And putting his arm round Danny he added, 'I don't need an official receipt for this piece of baggage.'

190

As a final gesture and at Danny's special request, the CSM and Alexander completed a lap of honour round the grass feature at the end of Ockenham Drive before leaving Melbridge. Standing by the bus stop, the eyes of the Selby family followed the great truck until it was out of sight, heading for the bypass and the West.

Danny quickly readapted to home life. Not only did he appear to have grown physically during his last term at Preston, but in the eyes of his family he had developed a new sense of purpose. His easy-going attitude of 'take life as it comes' had disappeared.

A long session with John Lucas who had always doubted the wisdom of the Highminster experiment, had ended with a decision for three 'A'-levels – English, French and Economics. At the same meeting, it was agreed that Harry Leng, in association with Jan Podolski, should prepare him to take the Grade Eight examination in October, the test being an essential precondition for entry to the Royal Academy of Music. Assuming he passed Grade Eight he would be ready for the RAM audition in the spring of 1978.

A more immediate requirement – the need to pay £12.00 still owing to Mr Bailey for Rosie's rocking chair – caused him to cycle to Abbotshaven for a talk with Jan Podolski at Chopin House.

He found the Professor in buoyant form.

'You need money? No problem, Danny. I, Podolski, enrol you additional member of Southern Counties Philharmonia. Ah-ha – you don't know?' The conspiratorial Professor rested his index finger against the side of his nose, as if he was about to reveal a profound secret. 'I, former Professor of Music, University of Cracow, am now entrusted with auditioning for orchestra. I declare you, Daniel Selby, have necessary qualification. Therefore you entitle yourself to small fee for each performance. Howzat!'

The Professor had belatedly been initiated into the mysteries of cricket – 'summer game, Danny, special appeal for poets and musicians.'

'But one small problem, my friend, Podolski plan needs small capital investment, namely cost of dinner jacket. Mr Joseph Selby pay tailor and you learn to tie black bow proper? *Top priority!*'

But Danny and his mastery of the bow tie played only a small part in the activities of the Selby family. Becky had enjoyed meeting

191

Jeremy Caxton's family in Sevenoaks. Kathy and Joseph found time to continue their golf lessons with Sandy MacNaughton who was kept extremely busy, not only as a golf instructor, but also as unpaid acting assistant secretary. Julian Grant had undoubtedly picked a winner in this Glaswegian, who was ready to accept responsibility and identify himself with the club's success as well as advance the prosperity of his professional business.

In July the course was open for play, though members were only allowed to use temporary greens and tees. But Bob Withers and John Mullins were well satisfied with the growth of the grass seed on the newly constructed greens and tees, and confident that the full course would be ready by May 1978, in accordance with the original schedule.

Meanwhile, prospective members were being attracted to the course, not only by Sandy MacNaughton's skill as a professional and the availability of the practice ground, but also by the provision of light lunches and early evening meals in the new club house.

Freddy Melchester and Bob Withers, the vicar and John Lucas were often to be seen on the course, while Joe and Kathy were making good use of the long summer evenings. Taken by and large, they were excited by the way their golf was improving under the professional's tuition.

The even tenor of Selby life in Melbridge was, however, interrupted on the last day of August by the death of Grandma Selby. She was a very old lady. She had been kept alive by the devoted care of Flora Pennington, but had been taking less and less interest in the world around her. She had even ceased to find any stimulus in condemning Joe's marriage to a girl who is 'not one of us', or in passing judgement on the wickedness of the world as reported to her by radio and Flora Pennington.

She was duly laid to rest beside her husband in the old Methodist burial ground, after a short graveside service taken by the local Methodist minister who used the words of the Anglican prayer book. Apart from the Selby family and Flora, the only other mourners were Isaac's old friends, Edward Baynes and Leadbitter Jones. There could be no grieving as Rachel was interred beside the man whom she had accompanied to Melbridge over fifty years previously. The small company could do no more than echo Job's final conclusion: 'The Lord gave and the Lord hath taken away. Blessed is the name of the Lord.'

After the few mourners had left in their cars, Kathy walked back across the road to the graveside. Her eyes were fixed, not on the newly dug grave, but on Isaac Selby's simple memorial.

Joe joined her and held her hand. Impulsively she turned to him.

'Do you remember, Joe? The last time we were here? The decision we made to keep and bring up the baby together? And you thought Isaac would be happy to have another grandchild?'

Of course Joe remembered. He had never succeeded in analysing thoughts that stemmed from that day of pilgrimage, but he knew that, for him as well as Kathy, the loss of the baby had seemed infinitely sad. Any lingering sense of guilt or relief had been extinguished by the brightness of the vision they had briefly glimpsed beside Isaac Selby's grave. Today, in this lonely place, they knew that hope and desire had been rekindled. No words were spoken as they returned to their car, but Kathy was aware of the increasing pressure of Joe's grip on her arm.

With Becky back at university, Joe and Kathy made a sudden decision to take a fortnight's holiday. Neither of them could recall who first suggested a break from the routine of Melbridge life, nor why they agreed, without any hesitation or argument, to return to that small magic corner of north Cornwall where they had spent their honeymoon and those early holidays with the children before Joe had become so absorbed in the development of his legal practice.

They would not admit to being swayed by nostalgia nor by some sentimental desire to recapture the joys of earlier days. They were twenty years older now, with new interests and more money to spend. They would need to take their newly acquired golf clubs with them and Kathy should be spared all cooking and catering duties.

A word with the knowledgeable Julian Grant confirmed that in north Cornwall they would never find a more perfect links course than St Enodoc which lay to the north of Padstow Bay and the Camel estuary. Julian also recommended a small hotel three minutes' walk from the club house – 'very well appointed and excellent cuisine.'

Sandy MacNaughton added some realistic advice. 'Mr Grant is

right about St Enodoc – no better holiday links south of the border. But ye'll be wise to play your golf on the short course. Walk the main course and get some of the grandest views of the coastline; but the climb to the seventh and thirteenth tees and some of those bunkers are a wee bit formidable for beginners.'

31

The St Enodoc holiday was a huge success in every way – the weather good, the wind light, the hotel excellent, and the golf club welcoming.

Joe and Kathy followed Sandy MacNaughton's advice and stuck to the nine-hole short course, which exactly suited their beginners' status. But Joe, mindful of his responsibilities at Melbridge Golf Club, picked up useful information from a friendly member, on the steps by which the main course was recovering from the drought of 1976; the plans for extending the short course to eighteen holes and the long lease arranged with the Duchy of Cornwall for the land on which the course was built – surely a perfect model which he could recommend to Freddy Melchester.

But Joe and Kathy also found time to revisit old haunts such as the bay where Joe had once saved the boy from drowning. Equipped for the day with a packed lunch, they felt sufficiently energetic to climb to the top of Tintagel and gaze with renewed wonder at the incomparable view of the Atlantic seaboard which this fabulous rock fortress commanded. Inevitably, they recalled the romantic adventures of King Arthur's knights, and soon they began to invent stories about the holy men whose curious names – Enodoc, Petroc, Miniver and Kew – were scattered over the map of this magic land.

Kathy would laugh at her map-reading husband.

'Joe, you've forgotten Breward, Malyn, Teath and Tudy – you haven't done your homework! Anyway, who were they? And who was so lavish with these beatifications?'

And Joe would cap her laughter.

'Alas, dear lady, the holy men could not write and left no records.

But Mr Joseph Selby, a notorious teller of tall stories, advances the theory that these men with the strange names were Welsh wizards, trained by Merlin, who escaped from the horrendous weather in central Wales by putting to sea in coracles. The lucky few who stayed afloat reached the Camel estuary. Once on dry land, they were welcomed by fellow Celts who turned them into saints on the basis that they were not only Welsh wizards but lucky ones too. How's that for a story?'

'A load of rubbish,' said Kathy decisively. 'But at least we can thank St Enodoc for favours received.'

Good news greeted the Selbys on their return to Melbridge. Leadbitter Jones reported that the planning authority had granted 'other use' conversion to four derelict buildings on the old Saxby's estate, and thought that Mr Joseph might wish to convey the good news personally to His Lordship.

At the new golf club, more original members were being recruited and Melchester businessmen were beginning to use the club house for light lunches.

Playing was still restricted to temporary greens and tees, but the earth-moving contractors had completed their work and Bob Withers and Mullins were delighted with the progress of the sown grass. Meanwhile, the professional was very busy, and reporting considerable interest from women attracted to the course by the special membership terms.

At 10 Ockenham Drive, Danny heard he had passed the violin Grade Eight test with Distinction which meant that he would qualify for an audition with the Royal Academy of Music.

And then, in November, Oliver Carstairs confirmed that Kathy had started a new pregnancy. Christmas came and went. At Easter 1978, to the delight of both their families, Jeremy Caxton and Becky announced their engagement. Kathy's baby was due in early June.

On the first of June Professor Jan Podolski shattered the calm of Ockenham Drive.

The Southern Philharmonia orchestra was on tour that month and due to give its annual concert in the Melchester City Hall. At the last possible moment, the management was informed that the young

196

Chinese virtuoso, who had been booked for the Tchaikovsky violin concerto, was laid low in Paris with a viral infection and unable to keep her engagement.

The Professor's great moment had arrived. Before any alternative arrangements could be made, he approached the conductor, whom he knew well, and persuaded him to let Danny take the girl's place.

'No problem, maestro. I promise. We have substitute on spot ... young Selby, maestro ... you know 'im, eh? Darling of orchestra ... knows concerto like back of hand ... plays it beautiful ... prefers cadenza favoured by Stern ... schoolmaster and father give permission ... I fix ... I, Podolski, Professor Emeritus of Cracow, give guarantee ... success assured ... big local interest ... total sell-out headline press ...'

The Professor was irresistible, unstoppable... A conference between conductor, Danny and Podolski reached complete understanding. The dress rehearsal with the full orchestra went without a hitch. All was set, except for one item on which the Professor insisted.

'Must have white tie, Danny ... full dress, white waistcoat are *de rigeur* ... must not look like black crow picked by chance from orchestra ... I speak father.'

Danny demurred. He would look a fool ... feel uncomfortable. But in the end he gave up an argument which could only distress him before going on stage.

There was not a free seat in the house. In addition to the normal ticket holders, Melbridge people were present in strength. Apart from the Selby and Hardingham families, Joe and Kathy spotted Freddy Melchester and Bob Withers, John Lucas and Harry Leng with a large grammar school contingent, and then they noticed that Roger and Diana Powell had joined up with Ratty and a party from Highminster School. Everybody, but everybody was there.

The orchestra opened with the Debussy favourite *L'Après midi d'une Faune*. It was well received, the orchestra relaxed, and the conductor left the stage.

Expectancy was rising ... you could feel the tension of excitement, as the lights in the auditorium dimmed. Suddenly, the spotlight was trained on the door to the left of the stage and the conductor emerged with Danny beside him, immaculate in full evening dress ... He was given a tremendous and generous welcome. He appeared tall and handsome, and apparently unaffected by the occasion. Melbridgians in the audience could hardly believe that this young man who was to play one of the most famous violin concertos in the world was the Selby boy whose debut at the grammar school concert had so impressed them only three years earlier.

The applause subsided, the audience went silent. There was a moment of fine tuning with the leader. The conductor waited – 'Take your time, laddie, there's no hurry.' And then unexpectedly, Danny handed his violin to the leader of the orchestra, walked to the side of the stage, took off his tailcoat which he left folded on a spare chair, and returned to centre stage. Smiling his thanks to the leader, he took back his violin and returned to his place in the front of the stage, resplendent in white tie and white waistcoat.

'Still the unrepentant non-conformist,' whispered Roger Powell to his wife. Danny, for his part, looked for a moment into the dark auditorium and a half-smile, part humorous, part confident and so reminiscent of his father, lit up his face. At that moment Kathy knew her son was playing for her and her alone.

Then he nodded to the conductor and the pure notes of the solo violin filled the hall, as the audience listened to the most memorable opening of all the classical violin concertos . . .

The music, interpreting the kaleidoscopic moods of its composer, rose to its triumphant conclusion. Later, the critics would write of the young soloist's deep understanding of the composer's temperament and of his technical skill demonstrated in his mastery of the cadenza – but it was the purity of tone in those opening bars which would never be forgotten.

After the first round of applause, with the orchestra also rising to acclaim the soloist, Danny left the stage with the conductor, retrieved his evening tails, and returned, properly attired, to receive further applause.

Offstage, the Professor was waiting for his protégé. He made no attempt to restrain his tears. '*Tour de force*,' he shouted. 'Magnificent. Oh, you bad, wicked Philistine boy, looking like scarecrow, determined not to take high road to fame.' And the Professor hugged the boy in an exuberance of affection.

There were others in the audience less demonstrative but equally moved by Danny's performance – but Joe's eyes rested on Kathy. She smiled at him.

'Time to move, Joe, I think we should get to the hospital right away and miss the rest of the concert.'

James Messenger and Oliver Carstairs, sitting a few rows back, saw the Selbys leave. They also missed the Beethoven Pastoral Symphony, and on the following day, Kathy gave birth to a baby boy.

In July the child was christened Samuel and baptised by Edward Baynes during the morning service in the parish church. On the evening of the same day something – perhaps the shared memory of those early meetings as members of the voluntary choir – caused Joe and Kathy to leave the baby in the care of his sister and godmother, and return to the church for evensong. As they walked home after the service the ancient stone seemed to derive new strength from the rays of the setting sun. In the Close there was a perfection of colour in the contrasting green of the trees and the mown grass. The little world of Melbridge was at peace and Joe and Kathy knew themselves to be part of that world. They knew that all was well.

From Edward Baynes' Diary, July 1980

Now that I have retired, I can write more freely about that crisis in the married life of Joe and Kathy Selby. The truth is that, three days before Kathy's return to Melbridge, I met Joe in the Close. Our conversation was short and sharp.

'Thought you and Kathy were having a holiday in the Lake District.'

'Had to return . . .'

'Had to?'

'Well, you see . . .'

Joe got no further. I wiped the floor with him . . . told him that, whatever his reasons, he was crazy to put the formation of a golf club and Fagg's difficulties before the happiness of his wife and family . . . and would he, for God's sake, revise his priorities.

That's where I left it. But when the distraught Kathy came to me to make her confession, I knew it would be wrong to tell her of my chance meeting with Joe. I could only pray that each, by the grace of God, might be given 'a contrite and an understanding heart'.

Soon after that came my retirement. Outwardly our little town has not changed very much in the intervening years. You will still find the quality shops in East Street as busy as ever, and enjoy the peace of the Close and the parish church.

But a lively community cannot stand still.

My wife and I have found it hard to leave our lovely vicarage on Southside, but, thanks to Joe Selby and Freddy Melchester, we are renting a small easily managed house on the Saxby's estate.

We are in close touch with the Selbys who are enjoying their golf and sometimes leave the two-year-old Samuel in our charge. I recently officiated at the wedding of Rebecca and Jeremy Caxton, who has become a partner in Selby & Leadbitter, while Danny is about to start teaching in Roger Powell's school in Sussex. An interesting decision. That boy had every encourage-ment, goodness knows, to aim for international stardom. I sometimes feared they let Podolski push him forward too fast, too often. But good sense prevailed. Danny has chosen to give rather than take. My old friend Isaac would have been proud of him.

There have been changes too in the Melchester ménage. The Court has been converted into residential flats. The Melchester divorce has been made absolute and His Lordship is living in a converted cottage. Bob Withers lodges with John and Kate Mullins while their pretty daughter, Susan, is working as a secretary at the golf club which appears to be flourishing. Rumour has it that His Lordship is often seen in Susan's company. Wasn't it Bernard Shaw who once said that a classless society would never be established in Britain until a belted Earl married the parlourmaid?

But I digress. Let me close with a story, vouched for by Jan Podolski and Harry Leng. They say that a northern symphony orchestra has agreed to give a first performance to Daniel Selby's Cumbrian Symphony. Diana Powell, who has seen the manuscript, has told my wife that it is very English and has an affinity with Dvořák and Vaughan Williams and Joe and Kathy have been informed that it is dedicated 'in gratitude to Rosie, the CSM and Mr Bailey'.

Enough, enough . . . It is thirty years since I was inducted into the Living of St Peter and St Paul, Melbridge, and I have never regretted that I followed Isaac Selby's advice not to seek further advancement. I have not despised 'the day of small things'.

Thirty years – it's a long innings by modern Anglican standards. Perhaps I've made a few runs. Who shall say?

In the last day, only a fool will boast about his own score.